Wheels for Walking

Wheels for Walking

A Novel

SANDRA RICHMOND

GROUNDWOOD BOOKS
HOUSE OF ANANSI PRESS
TORONTO   BERKELEY

Copyright © 1983, 2009 by Estate of Sandra Richmond
First edition published in 1983
Reissued in Canada and the USA in 2009 by Groundwood Books

Groundwood Books / House of Anansi Press
110 Spadina Avenue, Suite 801, Toronto, Ontario M5V 2K4
or c/o Publishers Group West
1700 Fourth Street, Berkeley, CA 94710

We acknowledge for their financial support of our publishing program the
Canada Council for the Arts, the Government of Canada through the Book
Publishing Industry Development Program (BPIDP), and the Ontario Arts
Council.

 ONTARIO ARTS COUNCIL
CONSEIL DES ARTS DE L'ONTARIO

Library and Archives Canada Cataloguing in Publication
Richmond, Sandra
Wheels for walking : a novel / Sandra Richmond.
ISBN 978-0-88899-866-8
I. Title.

PS8585.I38W5 2009   jC813'.54   C2009-903517-0

Cover design by Alysia Shewchuk
Cover photograph © Veer Incorporated
Photograph on page 223 courtesy of Jim and Mike Richmond
Design by Michael Solomon
Printed and bound in Canada

To Eddie

One

1

I HATE THIS ROOM. It's always cold and drafty and the sun never shines in here. Two hospital beds without covers stand in the center with a small table beside each one — the only furniture. On one the dark blue nylon sheet drawn tightly over the middle of the white sheet is supposed to make it easier for me to transfer myself from my wheelchair to the bed.

One more thing I can't do.

My eyes fall on a small bulletin board. It's the only thing permitted on the off-white walls. It holds my daily timetable, put there so everyone will know where I'm supposed to be, so that I won't miss any of my therapy classes.

Actually, for a hospital room it isn't bad, as long as you're only going to be here for a short time. They say I will be here at least a year.

A year in this room. I don't know whether I can bear it.

It's funny. All day long I can't wait to get back here, to be by myself in this room. But when I'm here, I can't stand it.

I listen to footsteps coming down the hall. I hope they'll keep going. They do.

Suddenly I want to leave. I want to be where Jake is.

It's nice having Jake for a friend. He's always good to talk to. He sees things as they are. He doesn't try to make me feel better or be strong. With Brian I always had to look to the better side of things. I couldn't let anything get me down. I had to pretend life was great.

Well, Jake lets me feel what I feel, pissed off at life and at the world. He feels that way too and says so. It's refreshing to be hard and gross and to feel sorry for myself. I guess it is a kind of release.

I wanted to believe Brian. To believe that everything would be all right. He told me that nothing would change, that our love would keep growing. He'd never lied to me before, but he lied to me then.

I'm glad he's gone.

One evening after I arrived at the Alfred Best Rehabilitation Center I was sitting in the day room with Brian and my folks. The day room is nice and bright. It overlooks the city from the third floor. There are a couple of tables for cards or games and about four groups of furniture where patients can visit with each other or with their friends and families.

Mom and Dad and Brian were all talking cheerfully, telling each other stories and trying to be funny. I was pretending to listen while I stared over at this paraplegic.

He was about twenty, with thick black hair that fell

onto his face. Even from the other side of the room I could see that his eyes were blue, almost transparent. His chair was tilted back in a wheely position and he was holding it there, balancing on the back wheels as he rocked gently back and forth, looking out at the city.

I had a great urge to hold my chair in that position, too. It looked so casual. But I knew I couldn't. You need your hands.

A somber-looking man came over and spoke to him.

The paraplegic looked up and sneered, "Fuck off. Can't you see I'm trying to enjoy myself? Alone!"

The room was suddenly quiet. He let his chair drop and with one hand turn he faced the door and rolled across the carpet into the hall. As he passed me he winked, and I could see a sparkle in his eyes.

A thrill ran through me and I smiled. I looked back at the man and noticed a Bible under his arm. I smiled again, and understood.

Mom and Dad and Brian just ignored the whole thing and went on talking and laughing. That's what they do when things get rough.

It's fine for them. They come and go. I'm the one who has to live here. They can pretend the problems don't exist because for them the problems are only part-time. I wanted to say fuck off, too. I was sick of people who felt sorry for me, who continually told me everything would be all right.

Everything wouldn't be all right, and I knew it.

The next day I was sitting in the line outside the cafeteria waiting for lunch. I was thinking about Jake Thomas, who I found out had broken his back in a car accident and was paralyzed from the waist down. He'd been drunk.

When I reached the counter I pushed my tray along in front of the food. There was a lady to help those of us who couldn't use our hands to pick up what we wanted. When I reached the end a helper carried my tray to a table where most of the young people parked.

The cafeteria was the main place for any socializing between patients. Our programs were so full that during the day we really didn't have much time off, and in the evenings there were visitors to deal with. But everyone had to eat. It was the one place we could talk without the supervision of a nurse or therapist.

I noticed Jake as he moved along the line. A helper picked up his tray and brought it over to our table. I was glad there was a space next to me and hoped she would put his tray there. When she did, I said hi and quickly looked down at my food. I became aware of my sloppy eating habits and concentrated on not spilling anything. My roommate, Sharon, sitting across from us, asked the usual questions.

"What hospital have you come from?"

"Memorial," Jake answered with a full mouth.

"What is your break?"

"Lower back."

"Car accident?"

"You got it."

I ate quietly but didn't miss a word. Jake said that in the two months he had been in the hospital he'd learned that all doctors and therapists were jerks and didn't know what the hell they were talking about.

"I'm getting out of here as fast as I can. This therapy is a bunch of bull." Suddenly he turned to me. "What about you, babe? What are they doing for you?"

I gulped down a swig of coffee from the cup I was balancing between my palms.

"I don't know, but it's better than nothing. I'm not much good the way I am right now." I didn't need to tell Jake that my break level was between the sixth and seventh cervical vertebrae. He could see by my useless fingers and the small amount of movement I had in my arms that I was a quadriplegic and had broken my neck.

"Well, you look okay to me." He smiled. I was mesmerized by the blue of his eyes. "Can I buy you a cup of coffee?" he asked as he put up his hand and snapped his fingers at the helper.

"One coffee, black," he said, peering into my empty cup, "for my pretty friend here."

"A fast mover," Sharon said. "Better watch out, Sally. He looks like trouble."

The boys at the table laughed and I felt stupid, but good.

* * *

I roll out of my room and down the hall to the men's wing.

Jake is looking out the window, listening to his stereo. He often sits like this, staring at the parking lot below.

"Hi, Jake," I interrupt. "May I come in?"

He turns his chair. "Hi, babe. Of course, but close the door behind you."

I close the door.

"You know we aren't supposed to have the door closed," I say. Jake looks at me seriously. I feel my pulse quicken. "Or have you forgotten that I'm a girl?"

"Hell, no." He winks. "With a body like yours?"

"What do you imagine they think we can do?" I can't believe that I am actually flirting.

"Come here and I'll show you."

Even though Jake is a good seven inches taller than I am, sitting down we look into each other's eyes. I have a long body. I guess he has long legs. I wonder what it would be like to stand up in front of him — to reach up and put my arms around his neck.

But it will never happen. I will never stand anywhere.

"I'd love to break some rules. Isn't it fun to feel fourteen again?" Jake smirked.

"I'll bet you broke a lot of rules when you were fourteen."

"Yeah, when I thought they were useless, which most of them were." His voice sounds bitter.

"There have to be some rules. If there weren't any

you'd have chaos. But I can't see how treating us like children is going to make this hospital run any better. If they used their heads they'd give us a little more responsibility and privacy. Maybe then we'd feel like we were worth something."

I know there have to be rules. I don't agree completely with Jake. But he was brought up in a small town, in a poor family. His parents both worked until his mother died, and then he had to work, too. He didn't do well in school so he quit. He's had to work hard all his life. To get any happiness he had to break a few rules. And now this.

I watch as he grabs the wheels on either side of his chair. He locks his elbows and leans forward, keeping his upper body stiff, and raises his behind off the chair. We're supposed to do this to relieve the pressure on our rears so that we won't get sores from sitting all the time. I don't have enough strength to lift myself so I have to lean as far to one side as possible, and then to the other. It really doesn't do much good, but I seem to have fairly good skin and never get any sores.

"It makes them feel good to act like big cheeses, especially the orderlies. They get a thrill telling us when to get up, when to go to bed and when to take a crap!"

He reaches into his pocket for a cigarette. When it's lit he flicks the dead match at the ashtray. It misses and falls to the floor.

"Sorry, did you want a smoke?"

"No, thanks."

A grin flashes across Jake's face. "How about something a little stronger?"

"No. I'm not ready to yet."

"Come on. Life would be a whole lot better if Jake could show you the light."

He rolls over to the stereo and slams a tape into the deck. Rod Stewart fills the room. The music is loud and clear with a perfect sound. I am overwhelmed by Rod's presence. Jake used all his savings to buy the best stereo there is.

He lets his cigarette hang loosely from his lips as he rolls back to where I am.

"I do want to, Jake, but not yet. Somehow, though, I can't think life would be any better. Maybe a little more tolerable, but not better."

"It will get better, Sally. Don't be so down on yourself. Take a look around this place. Things could be worse."

Suddenly I feel angry. "Look, don't tell me to compare myself to those with worse problems. It doesn't make me feel any better. Why should it? Don't tell me you've accepted this whole thing."

"No, but the doctors say this is it so I'm not going to cry out loud."

"I thought you said the doctors were a bunch of jerks, that they didn't know what the hell they were talking about."

"They are. As soon as I'm strong, I'm gone."

"Well, I don't want to listen to them. How do they know I'll never be normal again? Do they think they're God? I'm going to show them." I try to push down the lump rising in my throat. I feel tears forming behind my eyes.

I won't cry, I won't. I clench my teeth to hold them back.

Jake reaches over and gives my knee a squeeze. I can't feel it but the gesture is calming. Jake is the only one who still makes me feel special.

"That's my girl," he says.

"Oh, Jake, I just want to be normal again. If only there was a chance. I can't believe this has happened. One day you wake up and your life is over. I want to go back to what I was."

"I know."

"I want to go to college. I want to get married and have a family. I want to go skiing and play tennis and ride my bike. I want to run and laugh and dance. I want to wear nice clothes and feel pretty."

Jake moves his hand from my knee and touches my cheek.

"You are pretty. You can be happy. You can go to college, get married and probably have a family."

"My God, you sound like Brian," I snap.

He turns away and rolls over to the stereo. He flicks it off and turns to face me. Silence hangs between us. Then he speaks.

"I couldn't afford to ski, but I liked to hike in the

mountains. To be alone with the scent of evergreens, to listen to the birds. I loved to feel the early-morning dampness slap my face and search for the sun as it flickered through the trees. Do you know what I'd like right now?"

I shake my head.

"To wake up alone with you beside me in a small tent. I'd make a fire and bring you fresh coffee. I'd like to get out of this chair, too. But I'm afraid we'll have to find something else to do."

2

TEN MINUTES TO TEN. I'd better get moving. I roll myself down the hall and into the elevator. I push the square numbered button with my elbow. The doors close. There is one in front and one behind. I go down to the main floor. As the doors open, I roll out.

I turn into the receiving room and am immediately slowed down by the carpet. It's a large room with a desk at the end. On one side is the physiotherapy department and on the other the occupational therapy department — O.T.

For me, going from one end to the other is like crossing an ocean in a small rowboat. I can hardly move my chair. People who are waiting sit around the room and watch me. Sometimes they smile but mostly they look pitying. I hate it.

What a relief when my wheels reach the linoleum on the other side. I roll past the glassed-in office where the physios do their paperwork. Michael looks up and waves. I keep going over to the mats.

I pull out the armrest of my chair and replace it with

a flat sliding board that makes it easier to slide onto the raised mats. It has taken me a month to be able to get the board into the correct position.

Michael comes out of the office. He smiles when he sees that I'm ready.

"Hi, Sal. All ready?" he asks cheerfully.

"Sure."

Michael Harris uses time like a miser uses money. He makes every second count. Some physios can be distracted by idle conversation or a few moans and groans, but not Michael. He has so much energy he makes me feel tired. I feel as if I'm going backwards.

Right now I'd like to go backwards. Back to my room. But that wouldn't do me any good because someone would come in and when they saw me there, not at program, they'd look up at the bulletin board. It's marked *Physio—10:00-11:00—Michael*. Then they'd ask me what the matter was. I'd have to say I was sick. Then a registered nurse would come. It would go on report. Everybody would be angry. Wasting people's time is a very big offense around here.

Michael bends over and pulls off my shoes. He replaces my feet carefully on the foot pedals. Then he sits on the mat.

"Okay. Pick up your feet."

As he leans back on his hands I look at him. He's tall and good-looking. His skin is clear. He must eat well and get lots of exercise. I'll bet he's a skier.

"I can't." I look at my knees.

He doesn't say anything. He waits patiently.

I try to lean forward. I feel as if I'm going to fall into my own lap. I can't reach.

"Hook your left arm around the back of your chair."

I try, but I still can't reach.

"Try to slide your bottom away from the back. Throw your head back and push with your elbows. Look, like this."

I watch. I feel a lump growing in my throat. I throw my head back and try to push. My body slides forward ever so slightly.

"Good! Do it one more time." He sounds pleased. I feel like a child.

I do it again. But now I feel as if I'm lying in my chair rather than sitting.

"Now what?" I can't look at him. I feel foolish.

"Hook your arm around the back of the chair again. Pull yourself up into a sitting position without sliding back into the chair." He says it kindly but that doesn't help.

It's no use. I can't do it. My arm is aching from being twisted backwards and I can't pull myself up.

Michael comes around behind me. I can see he isn't going to let me quit. He pushes me forward so that I'm sitting up.

I am furious. How would he like it if someone pushed him around? I sit and wobble, trying to get my balance. My body feels like a wet noodle, totally out of control.

"Lean forward and hook your right arm under your right knee. Don't worry," he adds before I can complain. "I won't let you go."

I reach for my leg and hook the back of my wrist under it. I look sideways at his knees. "Now what?"

"Now lean back keeping your elbow locked. As you lean back your leg will come up. If you can, swing it over to the mat."

"Sure thing," I groan.

I fall back. As I do my knee comes up. However, my wrist slips and my leg goes crashing down on the foot pedal. I lie slumped down in my chair.

"Good work," Michael laughs.

I have to laugh, too. It's either that or cry. And I'm not about to start crying.

He makes me do it four times, and I begin to get the feel of it. On the fourth try I almost get my knee up, when I feel it slipping. Michael whips his hand underneath my ankle and lowers it onto the mat. He does the same with the other foot. I slouch back, exhausted.

"Now, lock your elbows at your side and lean forward."

"Oh, Michael, I can't. I'm too tired." Now I do feel like crying. I look up at the big clock on the wall. Only half an hour has gone by. "I can't do any more."

"You're not going to. I'll do all the work. I just want you to go through the actions. Now, lean forward, lock your elbows and try to take some of the weight off your rear. I'm not a muscle man, you know."

If only he'd yell at me, I could yell back. But he's always so nice, so patient.

He is too much like Brian.

He puts my hands into position. I lock my elbows and lean forward. With one easy motion he slides my behind over the sliding board onto the mat and helps me to lie down.

I've only been here a month, but it seems as though I have been through this set of exercises a million times. Michael calls them going through the range. They are to strengthen the few muscles I have left in my arms, shoulders and neck and to keep the ones that don't work from shortening and contracting.

The words are always the same, the muscle different.

"Push, push, don't let me stop you," he says while I resist. "Push, push, hold it, rest. Push, push, don't let me stop you, hold, rest." He probes with those long fingers, trying to feel a flickering muscle. "Come on, it's there, push, I can feel it. Once more."

"There's nothing there," I grumble. "This is a waste of time."

"You're not pushing. Come on. I know it's there."

"You're wrong. There's nothing there."

I hate to look at him. It's like when you go to the dentist. You hate the dentist for what he's doing to you, but the only place you can look is at him. You can't close your eyes because you have to make sure he doesn't do something horrible.

I have to watch Michael. I have to know if he's touching me and where. He can have my leg hung up to the ceiling and I wouldn't feel it.

I look at him. Even his eyes are strong — steel gray. I feel so useless.

I look at the clock. "I've had enough. Let me go."

"We've got ten minutes."

"I can't do any more." I close my eyes, hoping I'll fade away, cease to exist.

Michael reaches for my wrists and pulls my limp body up. I don't even try to hold a sitting position. I let my body fall forward onto my thighs. He goes around behind me, grabs the back of my pants and slides me backwards into the chair.

He doesn't say anything. Neither do I. What is there to say?

I hate him for knowing. I hate him for expecting things from me when he's just fine. I hate him for seeing me this way and not the way I really am. I'm a cripple to him, not a normal person. He expects me to accept and be happy, to appreciate how wonderful he is and what he's doing for me.

Well, make me walk. Get me out of this damn chair and I'll like you. But don't expect me to like any of this because I'm not going to.

He puts my shoes on carefully. We're both quiet.

"Getting your feet down is much easier. Be careful not to drop them."

God damn him. I won't beg for help.

I hook my left arm around the back to hold on and angrily drag my legs over to the side of the mat. They fall onto the foot pedals.

"That's a good way to get sores on your feet," he says in a matter-of-fact tone.

"Who cares?"

"I do." He turns and walks back to the office. "See you tomorrow," he says with his back to me. "I hope you're in a better mood."

I sit slumped and crooked in my chair, close my eyes and think of Brian. He wraps his long arms around me and I snuggle into his chest. We wrestle, our bodies bouncing against each other. He won't let me go.

Brian never held back his joy. You could always hear his voice above everyone else, and his laugh was like an echo. I loved to put my ear to his chest and listen to it from inside. He could always see the good in things. He had a knack for making everything seem all right.

The day my dog died, he took me down to the pet store where they had a litter of cocker spaniels. I picked one up and cried into his soft puppy fur. He licked my face and wriggled all over. Suddenly Brian and I were both laughing.

The thought of Brian's laughter fills me with a dull ache. I remember how he loved to go to funny movies. Afterward we'd repeat the lines, weave them into our conversations, then laugh all over again.

It's not only his laughter that I miss, it's just being with him. I miss our talks, the way he would listen to me and understand me. I miss our long walks on the beach, the wind blowing the hair away from our faces. Sometimes he'd chase me, catch me from behind, then spin me around. He would blow into my neck, and I would shriek with delight.

3

ON TUESDAYS AND THURSDAYS at three-thirty I go to see Dr. Ericson. He's a hefty man who looks as solid as a cement building. He has a square face, and his thick, neat, graying hair stands straight up in an old-fashioned brushcut. His greeting is always the same. "Good afternoon, Sally."

"Hello," I mumble.

It annoys me to come here. I like Dr. Ericson, and I feel more comfortable with him than with anyone besides Jake, that is — but I resent having my feelings put on a chopping board. Psychiatrists are for crazies and I am not crazy. Just because I get a little depressed once in a while they think I need help.

And who wouldn't get depressed? I know what's the matter with me. I can't walk. The way to make me happy is to make me walk. Talking about my feelings isn't going to make me any happier, so why bother?

He smiles at me from across his desk and puts down his pen. He has my life in front of him.

"How are you today?" he asks kindly.

"The same as last time," I answer, then wish I hadn't been quite so rude.

He waits for me to say something. I always find it hard to get started. My mind seems to go blank.

"I was hoping you'd feel a little better about coming," he says as he folds his hands and rests them on the file.

Oh, no, not another pep talk. Not from him.

"Do you have many visitors in the evenings?"

"Not anymore." I feel the emptiness that comes when I think of Brian. "Only my parents."

Ericson raises his eyebrows. "It doesn't sound as if you like your parents to come."

"I don't."

"Why not?"

"Because I can't stand the way they look at me. They look as if they're the ones who are hurt. It's either that or they pretend life is rosy. Sometimes I wonder whether it's me or themselves they're trying to cheer up. I know it's because they love me, but it doesn't help. I mean, how am I supposed to like this new me if all I do is make everybody unhappy? They always ask the same questions. 'What did you do today?' Well, I do the same things every day. I feel as if I should show them a report card. Mother always asks if I talked to the doctor. Doctors don't know any more today than they did yesterday. Don't they realize that if there was any great news I would tell them? Why do they always make me feel like a failure?"

I don't wait for Ericson to answer. I know he wants me to do all the talking.

"Also, when they come, they think they have to talk nonstop. I have heard more stories about relatives I didn't even know existed. And I've heard more miracle stories than there are in the Bible. They have absolutely nothing to do with me. And if they tell me one more time to have faith, I think I'll scream! I guess I'm ungrateful, but my mother sits around all day trying to think up things that will make my life easier. Then she comes and shows me all her inventions. Like last week she got Dad to make me some really thick wooden knitting needles. She proceeded to show me how I could knit using my teeth and thumbs. Can you imagine?"

"What about your father?"

"Dad's not too bad." A special warmth comes over me, as it usually does when I think of my father. "We seem to have a way of sharing our feelings without saying much. It's hard on him, though, because he tries to shelter both Mother and me. He has a better grasp of the whole thing, but he still feels sad."

Ericson writes something in his notes. My throat is dry from talking, and as I swallow the sound is loud in the quiet room. Neither one of us speaks for a moment.

"You said the last time that you felt trapped. Do you still feel that way?"

"Yes."

"How?"

"What am I supposed to say? Everyone around here is always asking, 'How do you feel about what has happened? Are you adjusting?' I don't know how many clergymen and social workers have come to ask me how I feel. Have I accepted? Have I accepted what? Do I know what has happened to me? Yes, I know. But am I supposed to stop hoping to recover? Stop praying to get better? If that's what they mean, no, I haven't accepted. And I don't want to. I have to have some hope. I don't ever want to think that this is it forever." I stop and drag some air into my lungs.

"Every time a nurse comes around she wants to know how I feel. If I tell her I'm pissed off about the whole thing it goes down in report — I'm not well. I'm depressed. They ask you something and if you answer them honestly, they label you. My feelings change. Sometimes I'm hopeful, sometimes I'm mad, but mostly I'm tired of people asking me how I feel."

I'm leaning forward. I can feel the veins tighten in my neck.

"What I really don't understand is why they have to ask in the first place. Can't they imagine what it's like? Do they honestly think they would accept it all? Am I supposed to be a super gimp or something? Can't they think before they ask?"

I lean back and catch my breath.

"Anyway, that's how I feel trapped. I don't want to

answer dumb questions that I don't know the answers to." My throat aches and I can hardly swallow.

I look over at Dr. Ericson. He's writing in his notes.

"That's fair," he says slowly. He understands. He knows I'm not talking about him. "What about the chair? Is it part of the trap?"

"Yes. I feel nailed to it. I try and try to get up, but I can't. Everyone told me at the beginning that it was just a matter of willpower, that if I really wanted to, I could make it. Well, I want to, but no matter how hard I try, nothing happens."

I keep talking so that he won't ask me any more questions.

"When I was little my big brother used to pin me down on the floor. He would sit on my stomach, put his knees on my upper arms and hold my wrists to the floor with his hands. He would lean over me and slowly get a spit bubble in his mouth. Then he let it fall on me. I would desperately try to move, but I could only move my head. I hated that feeling then. I hate it now."

"How do you feel about your brother?"

"I love Charlie. He was only teasing. I guess I was little and liked the attention. As brothers go, he's always been pretty good to me. It's just that feeling of being trapped that I hated."

He nods.

"Sometimes I wish he weren't so far away. But mostly I'm glad he's at school. He flew back from the university after the accident and I felt…ashamed. Oh, he was wonderful to me, but I felt as if I'd let him down. I always wanted him to be proud of me, and now I'm sure he wishes I were dead."

Ericson doesn't comment.

"That's what I hate about this place. I always feel trapped."

"Do you mean trapped by the building?"

"By the building and everyone in it. I can't even get up the driveway without getting stuck. If I did, where would I go? You can't go anywhere around here to be alone. If you go to your room there's your roommate or some nurse who wants to chat and see how you're doing. If you close your door they come in to check on you. God knows what they think you're doing. In the evening if you want to stay in your room and have a cup of coffee while you quietly watch television or read, they think you're becoming antisocial. You can't do that! You have to go down to the cafeteria. Sit around and listen to everyone else's problems. I've got enough problems of my own."

"Does everybody talk about their problems?"

"You better believe it. Everyone knows about everyone else's bladder and bowels — whether so and so had a crap today or not. And if you don't hear it in the cafeteria you hear it from the nurses or orderlies. Nothing is sacred. I never used to swear. I've picked that up since I've been here. It must be a side effect of paralysis. Not only that,

I've lost my sex along with its appeal. Do you know what it feels like to be a nothing? An uncontrollable mass of flab and bones?"

Dr. Ericson looks concerned. "You still look like an attractive young lady to me, and you're definitely feminine. I'd say your language is a little coarse, but it's natural to pick up what you hear."

"Well, it doesn't matter what you think. It's what I think that matters. How does that old cliché go? It's what's on the inside that counts."

"That's right. But nothing has happened to your insides. You should be the same person."

"Well, I'm not. I've become horrible! I hate myself."

"Let's talk about what you can do to be more like yourself."

Thank goodness he didn't say "we."

"What were the things you liked about yourself before? Is it possible to be like that again?"

What you say to Dr. Ericson is between you and him. I know he writes things down as we talk. But I also know that it's confidential. It's one of the reasons I like him.

I've mentioned Brian several times but have never said anything about him. I know Dr. Ericson wants to know more, to know what happened. I suppose one day I'll let it all out.

But not yet. I'm not ready.

4

I CAN'T BELIEVE I'M actually doing this. Brian would have a fit. I always wanted to try it but never had the guts to admit it.

Oh, sure, we talked about other kids using it. Brian said it was dumb. He couldn't understand what the big thrill was, messing around with your mind. He thought that if people had to use drugs to get their kicks they must be pretty low.

Well, I guess I am low. In fact, I don't see how I could get any lower and I don't give a damn if it messes up my mind. If I don't have a mind then I won't be able to think so much.

Anyway, Jake's been using the stuff for years, and if you ask me he's not scrambled. At least he knows who he is and what he wants from life.

I watch Jake take the thin, hand-rolled cigarette from his pocket. I want to imitate every move so I won't look like a fool.

He holds the joint between his thumb and forefinger

and takes a deep drag. Slowly he lets the smoke escape. He looks defiant as he draws in again. He hasn't said a word.

His wheelchair is parked close to mine, so he leans over and holds the joint to my lips. I'm glad because I've been worrying about how I would hold it. As I draw in through the hot thin paper, the smoke burns my throat.

Jake and I are sitting in the garden behind the gymnasium. There's no one else around.

It feels heavenly to be alone. The sky is a clear blue. I hold the sweet-smelling smoke inside and to my surprise my fingers begin to tingle.

I feel totally relaxed. Jake drags on the cigarette long and hard. He closes his eyes and holds the smoke in.

Finally, he holds the joint up to me again. The cigarette is hotter and the smoke tears at my throat. I put my head back and let the sun overwhelm me.

I remember a party that Brian and I went to where some of the kids were smoking dope. I mentioned to Brian that they all seemed to be in love with each other.

"Maybe we should try it," I said. "You might find me more beautiful and irresistible."

Brian reached around my shoulders and gave me a hug.

"I don't need any stinky weed to show me how beautiful you are, Sal."

"Here, do you want another drag or not?" Jake says. "Don't tell me you were off on memory lane again. This stuff is supposed to make you forget, not get all sad."

"I want to remember, Jake." I pause and hold the

smoke inside me. "It makes me feel better to remember that I haven't always been this way. It's as if I'm normal. In my dreams I'm never in this stupid chair."

"Listen, babe, you are still normal. Just because you're sitting down doesn't mean you're any different than you were before."

"Yes, it does and you know it. You can't tell me this is normal."

"Listen, Sally, I like you. I like you a lot and I didn't know you before."

I'm silent for a moment.

"Do you ever dream about me?" I ask softly.

"Hey, baby, I have the greatest dreams about you."

"In those dreams, am I walking?"

"My dreams are better than walking." He winks and slips his arm around the back of me.

"Seriously, am I in a chair, or am I moving?"

"No, there's no chair. Why muck up my dreams with a chair?"

"You see? If you cared for me in the chair, it would be in your dreams. But you don't. You're imagining me as normal."

Suddenly the grass is too green and the sky too blue. I feel top heavy and struggle to control my balance. My body rolls as if I'm caught in an undertow and being washed out to sea. I can feel tears filling my eyes, which seem as big as the ocean I am being dragged into.

"Hey, man, you've got it all wrong," he says, his arm

firmly around my shoulders. "The chair isn't in my dreams because the chair isn't important. It's you that's important. You're the one that I want to move with and be with. I may not do it like I want, but I can use my dreams to get me where I want. Thank God I've been there. I know where it's at."

His words make me gasp for air as I am pulled back with the undertow. Churning with sand and water I'm flung with the waves, breaking.

"Well, I don't know," I sob. My throat feels parched and sore. "I've never been there. I'll never know what it's like to love someone."

"Stick with me, baby. We'll find a way. There's always a door to heaven. We just have to find it."

Suddenly I feel heavy. I can hardly lift my arm to wipe my nose.

Jake tightens his arm around my shoulder and pulls me toward him. I let my head flop onto his shoulder.

"My head feels as if it's going to float away from my dumb body."

"Babe." I turn and gaze into his eyes, blue as the sky. I catch my breath. "You are a special lady. I want to kiss you and hold you and love you."

He pulls me as close as he can. He kisses me. I become lost in the taste of him. I try to keep believing that this is real. It's hard to hold a thought.

"I want you, too. But I don't know how." Tears cloud my eyes.

Jake kisses me again. I feel suspended in a daze. He forcefully pushes me back up into my chair. I straighten myself out as best I can. My eyes are hot and I know they must be red. He reaches over and holds my hand.

"You look awful," he says, "but beautiful."

"I feel awful." My face spreads into a huge grin. "But beautiful."

We burst out laughing. Everything suddenly seems funny. The world is the color of a rose.

Thank God I have Jake. How could I ever live in this zoo without him?

I watch Jake's lips as he tells me he has to go, that he'll be back later. I feel as though I'm far away from him but I know he's right here.

I don't want him to go. He looks tough with his thick black hair falling into his eyes. I want to reach out and touch the roughness of his face.

Jake turns his chair and speeds away from me. I can see his muscles bulging under his black T-shirt. If only I had my hands and his strength, then I could wheel like that. I could do so many things with my hands.

I slowly turn my chair around. I close my eyes and lift my face to the sun.

I can still feel Jake's arms around my shoulders. I can still taste his kiss.

Could I fall for someone in a wheelchair? Why does everybody hate him? I know my parents won't like him. Just the fact that he dropped out of school would be enough to turn them off. They wouldn't care why. Anyway, how could it work?

Why is my life so difficult? What did I do to deserve this? I never broke the law or hurt anyone intentionally. Maybe there were times when I could have been nicer to my parents. But parents expect their children to rebel sometimes. I'm sure they didn't want me to be a goody-goody.

I remember the night I sneaked out to go for a walk with Brian. It was a beautiful June evening and I thought I'd never seen so many stars. There were millions of them filling up the sky and each one was twinkling and shining like tinsel on a tree. We walked along, gazing at the beauty of it all and listening to the crickets sing. Brian had had a job working in the forest. He was tanned and smelled of the outdoors. It felt so good just to be with him, walking in the balmy summer air.

When we got back to the house I was glowing all over. He kissed me goodnight and then held me as if he didn't want the evening to end.

Mother was waiting for me when I slipped in the back door. Her face was all red and veins were standing out on her neck, purple and crooked. She clenched her hands.

"And where do you think you've been, young lady?" She tried to make her voice deep and strong, but it cracked halfway through. She was trembling with anger.

"I...Brian and I," I stuttered. "We were just..."

"Brian and you!" she shouted. "Brian and you. Do

you mean to tell me that you have been wandering around at this time of night with Brian? Where have you been? What have you been doing?"

"Nothing, Mom, honest. We were just out walking. It's the most beautiful night out there."

"Night. That's right. It's the middle of the night. How can you do this to us — to me?"

Suddenly I felt very angry. She never tried to understand. She always jumped to conclusions and thought the worst of me.

She started to pace back and forth. I stood and stared at her. I ground my teeth to stop the fluttering in my stomach and to stop myself from crying.

"Stop that!" she screamed. "I don't understand you, Sally. Ever since you've been hanging around with Brian you've been impossible."

"This has nothing to do with Brian. It was my idea."

"It was your idea! That's even worse. Get into bed this instant. I'll deal with you in the morning. And don't think this is going to be forgotten. I'm absolutely appalled." She turned and slammed the door behind her.

In the morning I sat at the kitchen table poking at my cereal. My mother had her back to me as she clattered dishes about. The kitchen was filled with her anger. I wanted to tell her it was all right, that I hadn't been bad, that I was just in love. I couldn't tell her I was sorry, because I wasn't. How could it be wrong to take a walk in the moonlight?

"I have been awake half the night." My mother paused. I stared back at her silently.

"Your father and I have decided that you are grounded for two weeks. You will come home right after school and you are not allowed out on the weekend. You can tell Brian about your punishment, of course. I would also like you to tell him how disappointed we are in him. I would have thought he'd have more sense." She waited. I said nothing. "I think you should know that I'm going to phone Mrs. Turner today. I think she would like to know her son is out prowling around at night."

I could feel the blood rushing up behind my ears. I stood up, scraping my chair against the kitchen door.

"You know, right now I despise you," I said. "You've made something perfectly harmless into something dirty." Gritting my teeth, I turned and walked out of the kitchen. For two whole weeks I didn't speak to her except when I had to.

Our anger toward each other softened with time, and the more she saw Brian, the more she liked him. I thought she finally understood.

But about eight months later, I told Mom that Brian and I were going skiing for the weekend at Star Mountain.

"That'll be nice, dear. Are you sure you won't be in the way? I thought the Bakers were having out-of-town guests this weekend."

"They are, so we won't be able to stay with them," I said cautiously. Mrs. Baker was Brian's aunt, and Mother knew her through the church. It was the only reason I was allowed to go for a whole weekend.

Mother looked up from her ironing. "And where do you think you are staying?"

"We're staying at the lodge."

"And who is we?"

"Brian and I." Quickly I added, "Joan and Barry were coming, too, but they both have to work this weekend. We've already put down a deposit."

Mother's face went pale and she put down the iron.

"Do you mean to tell me that you and Brian are planning to spend the weekend together in one of those cozy chalets?" She was trying to keep her voice calm.

"Mother, I'm almost eighteen years old. I think it's about time you learned to trust me."

"It's not that I don't trust you. It's just that I don't approve."

"Don't you like Brian?"

"Yes, but it's not Brian I'm concerned about. It's you. I'm sorry, but you can't go." She began to iron again.

I took a deep breath and said slowly, "I'm not asking your permission. I'm telling you what I'm doing. I'm an adult now and you can't tell me what to do." My heart was beating fast. "It's time I started making my own decisions. I'm going whether you like it or not."

Maybe if I'd listened to her none of this would have happened. Brian says I shouldn't think that way. I know he's right, but then why did it happen?

I remember Brian tall and strong. I can see him holding me in his arms, rocking me gently.

"I'll love you, Sal. Forever and forever."

"Me, too. Forever and forever."

I see us holding each other, but that can't be me.

Look at me. How could so much change in such a short time? I wish I could crawl back inside myself and be me again.

It can never work the way I am now. Oh, sure, Brian might still have those feelings for a while, but soon they would vanish. You can't love someone who is totally dependent on you. He would have to help me get up in the morning, help me get dressed. He'd have to help me around the house, if we could even afford a house. I certainly can't earn any money. He'd have to help me cook and clean, get things out and put things away. He'd probably worry about me all the time he was at work. I know he hates grocery shopping. What would be the point of having a wife like me, the way I am now?

A cloud passes over the sun and a chill runs through me. I feel sick and empty.

A group of wheelchair patients comes out of the gym and into the garden. I watch them struggle to move their chairs around the paved path. I hate to watch them because I see how I look. Except I'm even worse. There's no way I'll ever be able to move as well as they can.

I sit here, hating them.

Some of the patients are coming near me. I don't want

to talk to them or even look at them. I turn my chair and slowly inch toward the building.

My hate is like a blanket of wet sand, weighing me down. It is cold and suffocating. I have to find Jake.

5

IT'S FRIDAY NIGHT. Jake and I are watching television in Wally's room in the self-care unit. Wally, a friend of Jake's, has gone home for the weekend.

We both have Styrofoam cups. Mine is wedged between the thumb and forefinger of my right hand and held steady by my left. Jake balances his as he lights a cigarette. The vodka has been sliding down easily, and I feel lightheaded and silly.

"Do you think anyone saw us sneak in here?" I ask nervously.

"No, the place is deserted. How's your drink?"

"It's almost empty, but... I don't want to have to go upstairs so I can't let my bladder get too full." Then quickly I ask, "Where'd you get all this orange juice?"

"I always get extra at breakfast. If you'd come down to the cafeteria instead of being served in your room, you could collect some, too."

"Are you kidding? By the time someone got me up and dressed, breakfast would have been over ages ago.

Anyway, I'd just have to go back upstairs and get on the bed and take off my clothes again so that I could practice getting them on myself. My O.T. is always in my room right at nine to help me play dress-up."

Jake refills our cups at the sink. He sticks them between his thighs and rolls over to me. He hands me mine and lifts his up to a toast.

"Cheers," he says, grinning.

"Cheers," I mumble as I slowly bring my mouth down to meet the cup. The first sip is always the hardest.

Jake turns his chair around so that he can see the television and backs in beside me.

"Hey, man, a Western!" he says excitedly.

I laugh. "I bet you wish you were a cowboy."

"You'd better believe it, sister," he drawls.

We watch the movie silently for a while.

Up in my room I washed my hair on my own. I got water everywhere, but I did it. Having learned to dress my top half, provided that I wear simple things without buttons or zippers, I pulled my clean blue sweater over my head and even managed to put on a little makeup.

I look the best I can, I think, glancing over at Jake. He hasn't made quite the same effort, but he does look a bit like a cowboy, sort of scruffy and dusty. It's wonderful to know we're alone.

Jake sees me looking at him and turns toward me.

"How about a kiss for your ol' bartender?"

He leans over, I hook my arm around the back of my

chair and lean toward him. He nibbles at my lips. Then he neighs like a horse and makes me laugh.

Facing the set again, Jake slips his arm around me and gives me a little squeeze. I sip my drink carefully.

"How's your bladder holding out?" he asks when he notices my cup is empty.

"I'm sure it's full by now. But if I go upstairs they won't let me come back. It's ten and that's when they like us to get ready for bed."

"They don't bother me on the weekends," Jake says, "if they know what's good for them."

"Yes, but you can put yourself to bed. I can't. The late shift wants everybody in bed before they come on."

"Will they come looking for you?"

"I don't think so. They'll look around on the third floor, but that's all."

"Then don't worry about it. It's about time those night nurses did some work." Once again he fills my cup. "Maybe you'd better drink it straight."

"No. That would really do me in. I'll take my chances."

"Do you think this bladder training of yours will ever work?" Jake asks seriously.

"I sure hope so, but I doubt it. My bladder only holds about two hundred cc's. That means I have to get expressed about every two hours."

"Can you express yourself?"

"No. The nurses have to put their fist on my bladder and press down with their full weight. I'm surprised I have any insides left. They're probably all squashed together. There are only a few who can really do it. If they don't have the right touch, my bladder doesn't empty completely, so I have to get catheterized at least once a day."

"Will you ever be able to manage it yourself?" Jake asks.

I suddenly realize that I'm not even embarrassed to be talking about my bladder. Brian would never have asked me anything so personal, and I would have hated it if he did. We were both too shy. And I didn't want Brian to know about problems like these.

But I can tell Jake anything.

"I don't think so," I reply. "Dr. Spense says that maybe we can train my bladder to empty on a schedule if I follow a strict schedule for my liquid intake. I would get myself on the toilet at certain times and a small amount of pressure could release it. But I can't see myself getting on and off a toilet every two hours. I'd spend my whole life in the bathroom." I pause and take a sip of my drink. "Dr. Spense is going to teach me to catheterize myself. That might be easier, but not if I have to do it every two hours."

"Why don't you wear a catheter all the time?"

"It's so horrible. I can't bear to think about it."

Jake looks at me critically. "It would be a lot simpler. I wear a bag and I don't think I'm repulsive."

"But you're a guy and it's not so bad. You always wear pants anyways. I'd like to wear skirts and shorts in the summer. Wouldn't I look lovely with all that plumbing hanging out. And besides, it's healthier not to have a foreign body inside your bladder. Your catheter is attached on the outside, which makes it a lot safer."

"Hey, lady, so you can't be a cheerleader anymore. You shouldn't worry so much about what you look like. If everybody had to wear a catheter to empty their bladders it would be no big deal. The person who's making it horrible is you."

"Well, if I think it's horrible, I'm sure lots of others do, too. Just because you don't give a damn what you look like."

"You're right, I don't give a damn. I want people to like me for what I am, not how I look. If they don't like me and my equipment, they can go to hell." Jake reaches out and puts his hand on my knee. "Look, Sal, this bladder thing will work out one way or another."

I stare down at his hand and watch his fingers as they squeeze gently. I can feel him looking at me.

"You've got to be tough. There are plenty of beautiful girls who are a pain in the ass."

"I wasn't a cheerleader," I mumble, still looking down.

He slowly moves his hand up over my body. Reaching my chin he tilts it toward him. He leans over and kisses me. I feel hot and dizzy.

Jake pulls the armrest out of my chair and throws it on the bed behind him. He never uses one on his chair so there isn't anything between us.

"Put your arms around my neck," he orders.

I sort of fall onto him and fling my arms around him.

My right hand hits his ear before landing behind his head.

Jake holds me very tightly, and I bury my face in his shoulder. For a minute we hold onto each other.

Then Jake chuckles. "I can see why you weren't a cheerleader. You don't have much coordination."

"Shut up," I say, staring into his blue eyes.

"Okay, you're the boss," he smiles. This time his kiss is hard and passionate. I return it hungrily. He kisses my hair, my neck, and his lips are like fire against my skin. His hands find their way under my sweater.

"Can you feel that?" he whispers.

"Yes," I breathe. It's not a lie. I feel it with my heart. Just knowing what is happening fills me with excitement.

He slips his hand around my back and undoes my bra. My heart beats wildly as I cling to him.

We catch our breath and Jake snuggles into my neck.

"Do you think you could get onto the bed?"

I sigh, not wanting this to end but knowing it must, and push him away.

"No. Besides, Jake, it's late. I should really be getting upstairs. It's past eleven." I know that I'm wet but I don't want to mention it.

"I want to kiss you everywhere," he mumbles and nibbles on my ear, sending goosebumps all over me.

I laugh out loud. "There wouldn't be enough room for both of us anyway. These beds are awfully narrow. I'd fall on the floor for sure and then where would we be?"

Jake pushes me back into my chair and helps me pull down my sweater.

"Here, let me help you hook up," he says, rolling around behind me. He's so natural and smooth that I don't feel guilty or embarrassed at all.

He hooks me up and hands me my drink.

"You're quite a lady, babe. This is definitely one time when I wish you weren't in that chair."

I take a drink and a drag from his cigarette.

"Even if I could get onto the bed, Jake, what could we do?"

"We'd make love."

"But I can't move."

Jake looks into my eyes. "People aren't taught to make love. We'll just let it happen. Our lovemaking may be different, but it will be our way."

For a moment I let myself believe.

Suddenly the door flies open and an orderly looks in.

"Here you are, Sally. They've been looking for you all over the place. You'd better get upstairs immediately." He has a smirk on his face and I'm so embarrassed I want to die. He turns to Jake and adds, "You'd better do the same. You're going to find yourself sleeping on the street if you don't learn to follow the rules."

"Go fuck yourself." Jake almost rolls into him as he heads through the door. "Come on, Sal, I'll roll you home."

As I follow Jake through the door the orderly says, "If

I were you, Sally, I'd stay away from this guy. He's nothing but trouble."

No one is at the nursing station and the halls are dim and empty except for a few electric chairs parked by outlets, recharging their batteries.

I inch my way to my room. I don't want to wake Sharon so I take off my sweater in the dark. I fumble for my nightie and pull it over my head. I'm so glad that I've learned to do these things for myself. Somehow I don't want anyone else to touch me. I brush my teeth using the hand strap, and splash water on my face.

When I have my chair beside the bed, I pull the bell cord to call for the nurse.

While I'm waiting, I look at Sharon lying in the bed next to mine. Her back is toward me and her body forms a mound under the covers.

I like Sharon, but she doesn't like to talk much. And I don't want to push her. She'll talk to me when she wants to. Actually, I don't want to encourage her because I don't want to hear about her problems. I'm having a hard enough time dealing with my own.

We have a comfortable relationship. We're together and yet we keep to ourselves. The only person I really want to talk to is Jake.

I sit in the dark for half an hour before a nurse finally comes. Loraine is very efficient.

In a clear, crisp voice she says, "Well, I see the lady of the night has finally decided to come home." She gives the curtain one swift yank and it slides between the two beds, providing a bit of privacy.

"I've been here for thirty minutes," I say quietly, wishing she would speak more softly.

"I had to prepare the medications and then there was report," she answers in the same loud voice. I hear a movement in the other bed. "You know you are supposed to be here by ten. Do you need to be expressed?"

"No, I'm wet."

"Well, I don't doubt that." Loraine transfers me onto the bed and removes my slacks. I stare up into the blackness as she pulls at my clothes and pushes me back and forth. I hate feeling like a helpless baby.

"I hear you were downstairs with Jake."

I don't answer.

"You know, Sally, you should stay away from him. He's not your kind. You're a sensible girl from a good family. I don't understand why you hang around with him. He's nothing but trouble. Here, take your medication."

I swallow the pills. I want to say, "Because he cares for me," but don't.

She pulls the covers up over my shoulders. "Goodnight. I'll be back at two to turn you."

"Thank you," I mumble into the pillow.

I lie still in the darkness. Yes, I know exactly what Jake is. So we don't have the same background. Who cares? Right now I need him. He's the only one who makes me feel as if I'm still alive, that I'm worth something. He's so free. He says what he feels. Everything is less complicated because it's either black or white.

I remember his arms around me, his kiss. I never thought I could feel like that again. I try to relive every minute, touching him, smelling him.

I don't understand how they can tell me to stay away from Jake. Can't they see he's made me feel human again? Who are they to judge who my friends should be? It doesn't matter where any of us have come from or who we are on the outside. We have to look at what we are now. We feel each other's hurts and laugh about things that are tragic. If we manage through our pain to find someone, who are they to criticize?

Sometimes I feel so alone, so deserted by real life. It's as if the old me has died and I've been given this new, awful identity. I'm supposed to forget the old me and learn to live with this new me. How am I supposed to accept myself if they tell me not to accept someone else like me?

I don't know what's going to happen to me. I can't see the end of the road. I have to live for today and take each day one at a time. When we leave here we'll fit back into our old lives somehow — at least, isn't that what rehabilitation means?

Right now I love Jake and I'm going to hold onto him. I need him to teach me to be calm, to be myself. He needs me to keep him straight, to give him direction.

I wish they understood. I wish they'd leave us alone.

6

I'M LYING ON MY back with Michael kneeling beside me. He has his right hand on my shoulder and is pushing against me.

"Push, push. Push across your body. Come on, push, push. Rest. Now, push, hold it there. Good. Don't let me push you, don't let me push you. Good. Relax." He sits back. I stare up at the metal mesh above the mats that they use for hanging our slings.

We're like puppets held up by strings. The therapists pull and we move.

I wish I were made of wood. Then I wouldn't think or feel. They could paint a red smile on my face and make me dance.

"Okay." Michael smiles down at me. "Sal, my dear, you're now going to roll," he says, trying to imitate W.C. Fields.

But I don't feel like laughing. Every day I try to roll and every day I can't do it. If Michael takes my right knee and bends it, leaning it over my left leg, I can. But I can't do it without that leg up. If I'm ever going to be able to put on my pants I have to be able to roll. I can't always have someone there to lift up my knee.

"Swing your arms and roll on three. One, two, roll. Rest." A pause. "Try again. Swing, swing, roll. Rest." Another pause. "Throw your head together with your arms and shoulder. Come on. One, two, OVER."

I fall back on the mat. I'm not even close.

"One more time, Sal. You've got to use your head. I know you can do it."

"No, I can't," I mumble. "Use *your* head. Can't you see I can't do it?"

"Okay, that's it for today."

I give a sigh of relief.

Michael won't give up. "You've still got five minutes to get back into your chair."

"I can't."

He grabs my wrists and pulls me up into a sitting position. "Yes, you can."

Tears fill my eyes. I bite my lip. "I've got to get upstairs. I've got to get expressed."

"You've still got time."

I hate him. "No, I don't. The pressure will make me pee." My voice squeaks. "Michael, please. Not today."

Michael looks at me sternly. Then his face relaxes. "Okay, you win. But tomorrow we stop early and you are getting into the chair." It is a command, not a question.

I don't wait for him to straighten out my pants or pull

down my sweater. I fumble with my pusher mitts, turn my chair around and wheel away as fast as I can.

Once through the waiting room I turn down the hall. Tears roll down my cheeks and I think my ears are about to explode. The corridor is long and seems to slope to one side. I always have trouble going straight, but today is worse. I have no strength. My chair veers to the right and I crash into the wall. I bend my head and hold my breath.

Come on, Sally, get a hold of yourself.

I wipe my eyes with my sleeve and draw my arm across my nose. I can't blow it anyway, so why bother?

Why are you so stupid? Why don't you try? You're acting like an ass.

Michael makes me so mad. He's such a jerk. But tomorrow I'll do it. I'll show him.

I take a deep breath and let it out slowly. After trying to straighten myself out, I continue up the hall.

Jake is waiting for me by the elevator on the third floor.

"Hi, gimp! Do you want to come in for a little mood music before dinner?" He winks at me.

But I don't want to be happy.

"No, thanks, Jake. I haven't been to my room yet. I'll see you at dinner." I start to go past him.

He reaches out and grabs my chair.

"Hey, babe, what's the matter? You okay?"

I stop and close my eyes and nod.

"I'm fine. See you later." I push myself back to my room.

* * *

Today Michael isn't here. The therapist who replaces him leads me through the routine exercises. I ignore her attempts to make conversation. The hour drags.

"Can you get into your chair?"

"No."

In my room I sit and sulk as I stare out of the window, watching people come and go. I wonder if I'll ever be able to live on the outside again, if I'll ever make it. Who will help me? I don't want to always have a nurse around. Everyone says I won't, but I can't see how I can take care of myself. It feels as if I've been here for years, but it's only been a couple of months.

Five months since the accident. This can't be it. I can't be like this forever. I know God can't mean for me to stay this way.

I close my eyes and pray desperately, "Please, dear Lord, help me get out of this mess."

Then I think, Why should he help me and not all these other people? What's so special about me?

Nothing. I am just a nothing. I don't even try to do anything. I should have tried to get into my chair.

I watch people in the street. Maybe I don't want to get out of here. Maybe I'm afraid of what's out there. At least in here they take care of me. I'm not alone. I've got Jake, but what will I do when he goes?

Where was Michael today? I wanted to show him I

could do it. I wanted to try. I was ready. Why did he have to be away today?

I hear a nurse walk into my room. I close my eyes and pretend to be asleep.

"Sally," she whispers.

I don't budge. She turns and leaves. What a joke. Who could ever sleep sitting up in this horrible chair?

Where was I? Oh, yes, Michael.

I wonder what his girlfriend is like. I'll bet she's cute and lots of fun. I don't mean the beautiful type, but fresh-looking and a little crazy. I wish Michael wasn't so happy all the time. He's so much like Brian.

I remember the first day I saw Michael. He was sitting on the mats waiting for me. His short-sleeved white shirt was tight on his biceps, and his gray pants stretched across his thighs.

He isn't at all fat, just muscular. His hair is brown like Brian's, maybe a little lighter. He didn't make a big deal about me or ask any of the usual questions. Right from the beginning I knew he expected good things from me. He told me not to be discouraged, that things would come slowly, but they would come.

But I didn't want to be there and I didn't want to learn anything.

That evening Brian came to visit and I told him about Michael.

"He sounds like a nice guy," he said. "Maybe he could show me some of the exercises so that I could help you, too."

"There's only so much help I can take."

For a moment Brian looked hurt, but then he said, "Well, you tell him to keep his mind on business." He smiled.

A clatter of metal trays out in the hall brings me back and I know it's the trolley with dinner for those who can't go to the cafeteria. A signal for me to go downstairs.

The next day I take my time getting to therapy. As I roll by the windows I notice Michael speaking to one of the doctors. I feel a wave of relief and find a space on the raised mats.

By the time Michael is free I have parked myself, placed the sliding board and have my legs on the mat.

He doesn't say anything, just braces his foot against the chair to keep it from sliding away from the mat.

I slide forward in the chair. By now I know that wearing slippery pants makes it much easier to move. There is a nylon slipcover on the cushion and, with my new polyester pants, I slide fairly easily.

Leaning forward with my elbows locked, I try to lift myself up and slide over the board. I have to throw my head and shoulders at the same time as I push to get some momentum.

As usual I get stuck on the bump that goes over the wheel. I push and push but can't get over the bump.

Michael reaches over and gives me the slightest push. I slide onto the mat. Once I'm on the mat it is much easier because it's firm and I can get a better lift.

We go through the regular arm, shoulder, neck and

head exercises. We practice rolling, but I still don't make it. We work on improving my balance. Michael throws me a large, light rubber ball, which I try to catch and throw back. It's all I can do to hold onto the ball without falling over. Throwing it back is even harder, as I can hardly get the stupid thing past my feet. But I'm actually catching it without falling, so I feel good. I'm amazed at how much easier my movements seem.

Michael sits down on the edge of the mat.

"Okay, you've got ten minutes." It's evident that he isn't planning to help me at all. He doesn't smile but his gray eyes are calm, and I think how good-looking he is.

"Here goes." I look down at my thighs and lean forward on my arms with my elbows straight. I wiggle and push myself sideways to the edge of the mat, which is flush with my chair. By rocking back and forth, throwing my head and shoulders and pushing with my palms, I slowly slide backwards into my chair. I push myself up and sit back with a big grin on my face.

"You big fake," Michael laughs. "You could do it all along." He punches my shoulder. "That's my gal, Sal." He puts on my shoes and watches me while I lift my legs and place them on the foot pedals. I slip the armrest into position and he straightens out my pants.

Michael looks up at the clock. "You've tricked me out of five minutes."

"Too bad," I say happily and roll away, leaving him sitting on the mat.

I come across Jake sitting in the lobby.

"Guess what I did today," I brag.

"What did you do today?" he mimics.

"I got off the mats all by myself. Aren't I wonderful?"

"Can you get onto a bed yet?" he says, leaning in to grab my knee.

"No, but I'm working on it."

"Good. Let's go outside for a quick celebration." He spins my chair around so that I face the door. "Roll," he commands.

In the garden we find a deserted corner. The air is warm and filled with the fragrance of flowers. I breathe deeply.

"What are we ever going to do when summer is over?" I ask, watching Jake pull out a joint and light up.

He holds it up to me. "I don't plan to be around."

I draw in too much smoke and gag as it burns my throat. I try to cough and suck in air at the same time.

For a minute I think I'm finished. I can't catch my breath. Jake pounds me on the back.

"God, Sal, take it easy."

I calm down and wipe the tears from my eyes.

"Jesus," is all I can say.

Jake takes another drag and holds it up for me. "Take a short drag. You'll feel better."

"Jake, when do you think you'll be going?"

"In a couple of months, I hope. I really can't take this place too much longer."

"What'll I do without you?" Getting off the mat isn't important anymore.

"Hey, I'm not going to fall off the face of the earth. We'll work something out."

"Where will you live?"

"I'll get an apartment. By then I'll have my license so I'll come over and get you and we can get away from this place."

He has no idea. I'll never be able to get in and out of a car.

I watch him smoke. I shake my head when he offers it to me.

"When you finish here you can come and live with me," Jake says.

"Who will look after me?"

"I will."

"Come on, Jake, be realistic."

"We can get a nurse to come in. We'll work it out."

"How will we live? What kind of job are you going to be able to do? I'm certainly not going to be able to earn any money."

"The government will help us. Look, man, I live from one day to the next. That's the way I am."

You're right, I think. That is the way you are. That's one of the things I like about you. But I'm not like that. I want to know what's going to happen to me. I want to have some kind of life to look forward to, to work hard for.

"I want to go to school, Jake."

He looks at me curiously. "What for?"

"I've always wanted to go to college. Other people have done it in a wheelchair. I know it'll be hard and probably take me a lot longer than usual, but it's something to work for."

"People with big degrees think they're better than other people." Jake runs his fingers through his hair, pushing it out of his eyes. "Hey, if you want to go to school, why should I care? If you want to do it, do it." He takes a last drag on the joint and flicks it into the flowers. We both stare at the spot where it lands. The marigolds are bright yellow and orange balls.

Jake breaks the silence. He reaches over and pulls me to him.

"I'm proud of you," he says and kisses me on the cheek. "All by yourself?"

I am glad to change the subject and return his kiss. "All by myself. There's no end to the miracles of a gimp."

I had felt him slipping away and the thought frightened me. I hold him, not wanting to let go.

7

Dr. Ericson shakes his head.

"Why can't you look at yourself positively? You have such a bleak image of yourself."

I'm surprised. Ericson sounds almost angry. He's always so controlled. Am I trying to provoke him?

I look at him and suddenly feel guilty. I'm wasting someone's time. Yet somehow I want him to understand.

I begin speaking very quietly.

"There are so many things I can't do and won't ever be able to do. They overwhelm me. The few things I can do don't seem important. I don't try to sit and feel sorry for myself. I just can't see over the hills. I can't see over them so I sink to the bottom of the valley and the hills close in on me. I feel as if I am drowning in my own sadness. Everywhere I look I'm reminded of what's happening. It may be a small help to know that it's happening to the others, but that's depressing, too. I feel guilty using people who are worse off than I am to feel better. That makes me feel rotten. If only I could get out of here I wouldn't have to keep seeing people who remind me of me. But even if I escape I won't be able to do anything. You see, there's no way out."

My throat feels as if it's closing up. I swallow to try and clear it.

"You know, the other day a friend told me she was in an accident. The car turned over and she got her head stuck in the window. All she could think of was breaking her neck and ending up a quad like me. I can understand her feeling that way, especially after visiting me and seeing all the others in here. But how do you think I felt when she told me that the most horrid experience she could imagine was becoming like me? And one time a nurse told me how she'd been crossing the road and a car had rushed past her, knocking her down. She said she got to her knees right there in the street and thanked God she was all right. She said, 'I'd rather be dead than end up like you.' If I'd had a gun I think I would have shot her. Except, of course, I wouldn't be able to pull the trigger."

Ericson sits still for a moment, then shifts in his chair.

"I find it hard to believe that a nurse would say that to you."

"Well, she wasn't a real nurse. She was an aide. She may have felt that way, but why did she have to tell me?"

"Have you ever told these stories to anyone else?"

"No, because I know they're right, that I would feel the same way."

Ericson leans back. He spreads his fingers apart and

bounces his fingertips against each other. "Of course you were upset and hurt. A terrible thing has happened to you. And you are angry. It's good for you to see that you're angry. Once you accept that, you can begin to move on. You can't go on being angry forever."

"It's fine for you to say that. You can fit me into little slots and say, 'She's progressing. She's coming out of stage three, self-persecution, moving into denial of God.' But other people don't understand. They think I should be tough and brave. That I can lick this if I fight it. You won't believe how many people have said that if I really want to I'll walk again. My God, what do they think? Also, I'm supposed to have a sense of humor. Look to the good things. Well, I don't see any good things."

"Sally, no one is happy about what has happened to you. And I don't really think anyone expects you to be happy—"

"Yes, they do."

"Who?"

"My old boyfriend. He expects me to smile and carry on."

"Would you like to tell me about him?"

"No. What's the point? You already know about him anyway." I look straight at Ericson, my eyes holding his. He smiles and breaks the stare.

"Yes, I know who Brian is, but I'd like to hear about him from you."

"There isn't anything to tell. It's over."

"How long were you going together?"

It seems as if I've known Brian all my life. It's hard to remember back before him.

"About twenty months," I say quietly.

Suddenly Brian is in my mind. I can see his handsome face, his sparkling blue eyes, his lovely white teeth. I can feel his presence surround me, his strength making me feel protected, taken care of. Yet at the same time he seems so far away, as if he were a part of my past a long time ago. I want to reach out and draw him closer, but as I do his image fades.

"Was he with you in the car?"

"No, I was alone."

"How do you feel about that? Do you feel angry because he wasn't with you?"

"No," I gasp. "I don't want him to be hurt. I'm angry that it happened to me, not that it didn't happen to him."

"What about Brian? Can you remember how he reacted when it happened?"

Of course I remember. Brian kept saying everything would be all right. That it would take time but that we would make it. He told me I had to be strong, that I couldn't let myself get down. He wouldn't let me be angry.

"It doesn't matter. He's gone now and I'm glad. He's got his whole life ahead of him and he doesn't need me to muck it up."

"Did you love him?"

I can feel tears in my eyes. I swallow hard to keep them from falling.

"Yes."

"What does love mean to you?" I know Ericson is serious, that he won't lecture me about love. He's treating me like an adult.

But what can I say? How can I put that feeling into words?

"Do you still love Brian?"

"No." The word feels like a knife. "Besides, what kind of life would he have with me? There's no reason for him to give up his life."

"Do you still want to make him happy?"

"Yes, and the easiest way is for him to stay as far away from me as possible. I can't do anything for him. I would only be a burden to him for the rest of my life."

"Of course, those are things that you have to decide for yourself. I think you have many things to offer, and a great deal to share with someone. But it won't do you any good hearing it from me. It's something *you* have to make a decision about. When you can see that perhaps you won't be so angry."

"You tell me I have to accept myself the way I am. That there's nothing the matter with being a quadriplegic, that I can live a normal happy life, but that I've got to like myself. Well, I don't see how I can tell myself I'm okay when it's obvious I'm not. I know how other people look at me. I know how I looked at cripples when I was normal."

"Do people around here look at you that way?"

"No. They're used to us. But that's their job. There's some like that nurse's aide, but on the whole I'd say no."

"Maybe you feel guilty about what you thought of people who were in wheelchairs before."

"Yes," I say, "I have felt guilty. I remember every gimp I ever saw and how I avoided them and turned my eyes away."

Ericson writes something in his notes and then puts down his pen neatly.

"I want to talk to you about the word 'gimp.' You call yourself and others gimps. Some people find that quite offensive."

I look at him. "Well, that's tough. It's better than calling myself a cripple. Gimp is a nice word, sort of friendly. When you refer to someone as a gimp, people laugh. The word cripple reeks of pity. Anyway, you're the one who said I had to learn to see the funny side of things."

"That's right, and it's fine to use words like gimp around here because everyone understands. But people on the outside are embarrassed by it. When people get uncomfortable they tend to stay away."

"We've already established the fact that people on the outside stay away. They're afraid they might catch something or that we're crazy. That's what we're talking about. I know how normal people look at me."

"Sally, it's up to you to make people realize what you are. Most people don't know how to handle the situation. You're going to have to be tolerant of them and show them how. If you give people time you'll see that they like you. When you start realizing that there are lots of people who will look at you first as a person and like you for what you are, then it will be easier for you to like yourself."

I know that Ericson has said more than he wanted to, and I'm glad.

"Well, I'd rather have people shy away than hang all over me feeling sorry for me."

"So, you'll have to show them that they don't need to feel sorry for you."

"The only way to do that is to get rid of this chair."

"Fine. If you can do that we'll all be pleased."

I look at his tired face with the loose skin bagging under his eyes.

"But I can't help you get out of that chair," he says. "I can only help you learn to live with it."

"Thanks a lot." I turn and roll toward the door. He waits for a moment and then, without a word, he gets up and opens it for me.

8

I'M GOING TO WORK harder in physio. Surely Michael can make me strong.

I go to the department early to watch other people. Most of the exercises and routines they do are similar to mine and I am aware that they look like me.

Who am I trying to kid? I'm never going to be able to walk again. None of us is.

Suddenly I want to leave. I turn, then see Michael coming toward me.

How can I get out? I can't stay in here with all these people.

"Michael, can we go outside today?"

He tilts his head. "I know it's a nice day, but you have plenty of time to sit in the sun. We'll never get anything accomplished outside."

I'm desperate. "Please, Michael. I can't get around the loop because I'm afraid of the hill. You told me yourself that wheeling is the best way to build up my shoulder muscles. If you could help me then I could practice going around the loop on my spare time. Please."

"Okay," he says, "but you're going to work. Get rolling."

Out by the loop Michael sits on the bench. He stretches his long arms along the back and crosses his legs. He lifts up his face to the sun.

Who'd have ever thought such a simple act would make me envious?

"Hey, Sal, this was a great idea."

I start around the loop. There is a slight incline for the first thirteen yards so I put on my hill aids — little levers below the brakes. With them on I can stop without rolling backwards.

I stick my thumbs inside the rims of my wheels and push hard to get up the gradual incline.

Once around the top of the loop I come to the steep part. It isn't really steep, but I'm afraid to go down.

I stop.

"Come and get me."

"No, come here yourself."

"I can't. I'll go too fast."

"Put on your brakes."

"I can't reach. I'll fall forward. My arms are too short."

"Your arms are perfect. Hook one around the back." Michael tilts his head back to catch the sun and closes his eyes.

"You're a creep!" I yell.

"I'll leave." He stands up and turns toward the building.

"Don't, don't!" I push the left brake on halfway and

hook my left arm around the back of the chair. I lean forward and with my right hand I release the right brake.

"Michael," I cry as I roll toward the bench. I slam the right brake down hard and the chair swerves to the right and smashes into the bench.

"What a chicken," he laughs.

"You would be too if you always felt as if you were going to fall over. What if I fell out on the ground?"

"I'd pick you up."

"I don't always want to have someone with me."

"You won't have to. You'll learn what you can do and what you can't." He leans back and crosses his arms on his chest. "And rolling down this little hill is one thing you can do."

I know he's right. His eyes are bright and smiling. I'm suddenly aware of how attractive he is. I want to touch him.

I look down at my toes.

"I'm sorry I called you a creep. I didn't mean it." I slowly look up at him and see that he understands. His cheeks are pink from the sun.

"Tell me about your girlfriend," I ask shyly.

"What would you like to know?"

"Is she pretty?"

"Sure."

"She's lucky, you know."

Michael laughs a little nervously. "Well, I've always

thought so." Then in a different tone, "Enough of this stalling. Around the loop one more time."

"Do I have to?"

"Yes."

What a dummy. Now he probably thinks I'm madly in love with him.

He's so much like Brian, always answering a personal question with a joke. Jake is different. He levels with you, lets you share his feelings.

If only I could have talked more openly with Brian.

Thoughts tumble around in my head and I'm hardly aware of how quickly I roll around the hill. This time I let myself go and crash into the bench.

"You're right, this is a snap," I announce.

"I'll walk you to the gym." Michael stands up but doesn't try to push me.

You are a creep, I think, but I like the surge of independence that lifts me as we go along slowly, side by side.

In my room, I sit waiting to go down for supper. From my window I can see the physios and O.T.s leaving for the day. I wonder how they feel leaving us all behind to hospital food and boredom while they go home to normal life. Do they ever feel guilty, or do they feel glad to get away? I wonder if they think about us when they're at home, sitting in the sun with a cool drink and their feet up.

I watch their backs as they cross the street and go into

the parking lot. I look for Michael's car. It's funny that I've never noticed where he parks.

I think of Michael's face, his soft laugh — but mainly it's his strength that I love.

My smile turns to a frown and I shake my head. When did I stop hating him? I wonder how I could ever have hated him.

Maybe I've been so angry that I haven't let any other feelings come through. I care for Jake, but now I want Michael's friendship and help, too.

I wonder what he thinks of me.

Michael has his own life, and when I've left here I'll only be a patient he once treated.

I watch the cars as they drive away. I hate this feeling of being left behind. First Brian, soon Michael, and there's no way Jake could take me with him even if he wanted to.

Tears roll down my face.

I reach over to the drawer that is part of the built-in desk. Slipping my fingers through the looped handle, I pull the drawer open. In it there is a pile of pictures. I push at the photographs, scattering them around.

Halfway down the pile is a picture of Brian. Through my tears I can see his smiling face. I slip the picture between my forefinger and middle finger and slowly lift it out onto my lap.

I try to touch the picture with my numb baby finger.

"I wonder where you are," I whisper out loud.

"Whether you've found yourself a normal girl, someone you can be happy with."

I think of the night he left, and suddenly I can't hold back the tears. My chair rocks as I cry.

Two

9

I COULDN'T BELIEVE HOW lousy I felt. I sat in the kitchen leaning forward with my elbows on the table, holding my head in my hands as I watched Brian fixing one of the buckles on his ski boot.

It was unusual for us to be alone. Brian and Barry lived with another guy in a small apartment. It was an old building but well cared for, and from the living-room window there was a peekaboo view of the city.

Brian's eyes were dancing as he chatted away to the boot.

"Okay, baby, be good to me. That's it. I want you to make me look good now." He slowly twisted the buckle into place. "Atta girl. With you on my feet and Sal here at my side, I'll be the best on the hill." He looked up happily. "Swish, swish," he said as he dropped the pliers, threw up his hands as if he were holding his poles and jumped forward a little to land in the perfect position. "Swish."

I laughed halfheartedly. "If you look as good outdoors

as you do in here, you're bound to be the best on the hill."

Brian reached over and pulled me up. "Come with me to the couch and I'll let you tell me why you don't seem as happy about the weekend as I am."

He put his arm around me and I nestled into him.

"Well?" he asked.

"It's Mom. She's not very happy about us going to 'a cozy chalet,' as she calls it, all by ourselves."

"That's because she knows I'm lusting after your body." Brian pulled me close and kissed my neck.

"Be serious. She's really not happy."

"Okay, Sal. What did she say?"

"Well, I told her we couldn't stay at the Bakers', which she already knew. She wanted to know where we were staying so I told her."

"You didn't have to tell her we would be by ourselves."

"What if she saw Joan or Barry in town?"

"You could have said there would be others there. I mean, there will be, lots of others. They just won't be in our room."

"I'm not going to lie to her."

"You didn't have to lie. You just shouldn't have told her."

"She asked. I guess I wasn't prepared."

"Well," he said impatiently, "what did she say?"

"She said I couldn't go."

"Great, just great," Brian said angrily.

"It's all right. I told her I was going whether she liked

it or not. She's got to realize that I'm old enough to look after myself. She's never going to be happy about it, so now's as good a time as any."

"I don't think we should go now. At least, you shouldn't go."

Suddenly I became angry. "What do you mean?"

"You'll be worrying about it all weekend."

"Hey, I can handle my mother, and I promise you I won't worry." I already had my mother mad at me. I didn't need Brian mad, too. "We've been planning this for so long. We have to go."

"I don't know. We could ruin everything over one lousy weekend."

"Lousy! The forecast is for new snow. The powder will be super. For the first time we'll have a little privacy. Besides, I've already told her I'm going."

One thing I'd picked up from my mother was the ability to sound final.

Brian and I sat quietly staring out the window at the city lights twinkling in the distance. I slipped my arm through his and drew him close beside me.

Leaning my head on his shoulder, I said, "We have to go. Mother will come around. It's just that she's afraid I'll get hurt. It's hard for her to see that her little girl can really be in love." I spoke these last words softly. "Once she sees that I'll still be Respectable Sally, I'm sure she'll understand."

"I guess it's hard for parents to watch their children

grow up." Brian slipped his arm around my shoulders and drew me to him. "Especially when they know what's on our minds." He laughed like a demon and swooped down to kiss my neck.

Giggling, I pushed him away.

"You see, this is the whole point. We don't have to go away for the weekend for something to happen. It can happen right here. And to keep my mother happy, I'm leaving."

I picked up my parka and purse and headed for the door. I turned to Brian, blew him a kiss and said, "See you Friday."

* * *

The drive to Star was slow and treacherous. It had begun to snow and there was a slippery film on the road. I watched the large flakes form patterns on the windshield before being swept away by the wipers. It was fascinating to think that these delicate particles could pile up to make thick snowdrifts.

Brian looked straight ahead as he concentrated on the road. His fingers were wrapped tightly around the steering wheel and his body was stiff and alert. His MG was a good car and he handled it well. We had traveled this road so many times that he knew every curve and hill.

"You know, one of these days I'd like to drive up here in the daylight. It's such a beautiful drive and we never get to see it because it's always dark," I said, staring past him into the night.

"You may get a chance this weekend. If this snow keeps up we won't get much skiing in. We may have to drive down on Sunday afternoon."

I reached over and put my hand on his knee.

"Do you think we'll ever be able to own a cabin?" I asked.

"It would be nice."

"I can't think of a better way to spend our money. If we get our kids interested in skiing, we can spend the rest of our lives together as a family. We wouldn't have to worry about them hanging around the streets or getting mixed up with the wrong crowd."

"Sal, how many kids are you planning on having, anyway?"

"I think two would be perfect." I began to hum the tune "Tea for Two," and he joined in. "'A girl for you, a boy for me.' How about you?"

"As many as we could afford. I'd love to have a large family, but only if it wasn't a struggle to do things with them. But I hope you aren't in any big hurry. There are a few things I'd like to do before we get tied down."

"Yeah, like what?"

"Like get to the mountain."

The snow was falling more and more heavily. Brian leaned closer to the windshield.

Finally we saw the cabins hiding in the woods, their A-frames poking up among the trees.

We drove carefully through the small ski village until

we reached the lodge. It was a wooden two-story building with a large square in front. The lot was filled with
parked cars topped with ski racks and mounds of new
snow. Brian drove into the first empty spot.

I pried myself out of the small car. My boots crunched
on the frozen ground as I stretched my arms up to the
softly falling snow. The flakes fell wetly, melting against
my face.

I clutched my suitcase tightly as we made our way to
the front of the building.

"Brian, isn't it beautiful! Look at the trees. I love it
when the snow makes them droop like that."

Inside the lodge I suddenly felt a little self-conscious.
I had never stayed anywhere with Brian all by myself.

The clerk looked straight at me. I knew millions of
unmarried people stayed here, but I looked so young.
What if he asked if we were married?

I knew my face was flushed so I turned my back to the
desk. Fidgeting with the birthstone ring my parents had
given me, I turned the stone into my palm so that all that
could be seen was a slim gold band.

"Come on, Sal, we're on the top floor," Brian said
eagerly.

"Great." All the rooms opened onto a balcony that
overlooked the main lounge. As we went to our door I
felt that everyone was watching us. I couldn't get inside
fast enough.

"What's the matter? You seem a little edgy." Not waiting for an answer, he added, "Hey, this is great!" He plunked himself down on one of the queen-sized beds. "I love all this wood."

"Joan and Barry would have loved it," I said, wishing they were here.

"Sal, you don't seem very happy for someone who was jumping up and down a few minutes ago."

Looking at some of the photographs of local skiers on the wall, I began slowly, "I guess I feel a little funny."

"Aren't you feeling well?"

"No, I feel fine. I mean, it's just that...what do you think that man thought about us staying here by ourselves?" I kept looking at the pictures.

Brian laughed. "So that's it. You're embarrassed to be seen with the likes of me."

"Don't be a dummy. You know what I mean."

"All that man cares about is whether or not he gets paid for the room. Besides, he thinks there are going to be four of us in here. He gets young people all the time."

"I'm glad he thinks Joan and Barry are here."

"I thought you weren't going to worry about your mother?"

"My mother! I'm not worried about my mother."

"Well, you're worrying about the same thing she is. You might as well worry about her."

"I'm not worrying about anything. It's just that I feel a little self-conscious."

I looked at Brian lying comfortably on his back, his

hands behind his head, a big grin on his face. Why was I so nervous?

I looked at the two beds. What would happen later?

I knew my mother was worried about me even though I had tried to tell her there was nothing to worry about. I did love Brian, but I wasn't ready for anything like that. It wasn't that I was afraid of getting pregnant or catching VD, even though thinking about them gave me the creeps. I wasn't afraid of sex, either. I just didn't want it yet. I guess I wanted it to be special and the right time had never come. A lot of my girlfriends would have jumped at the chance.

"I'll go down and lock up the skis," Brian said, jumping off the bed.

"Sure. If I'm not here when you get back I'll be downstairs."

In the lounge I sat staring into the fire, my book open on my lap, thinking of Brian. I wondered whether we would have sex. I didn't know how I felt about it anymore. I couldn't believe that I was actually considering it. I wondered if Brian was thinking about it, too.

It was that room and those beds and the fact that we would be by ourselves all night. At home there was always the chance that someone would come around, and besides, it would never occur to me in my parents' home. And cars seemed so cheap.

I didn't think I was in any great hurry. I guess I'd never come this close before. Whenever I got together with my friends we would have these big discussions about virginity and marriage. I'd always agreed with them about losing it before. I mean, Brian wanted to do a lot of things before we got married, and so did I.

All of a sudden I wished we were at the Bakers'. They had such a great setup. The boys had their room, the girls had theirs. We all threw our sleeping bags down on the mattresses and there wasn't a problem about who slept with whom. Of course, we always wanted to be alone, but now I wished we were there.

My eyes wandered from the fire. Brian was coming along the balcony. He waved when he saw me and hurried down the stairs.

"Hi, love," he said cheerfully. "How's the book?"

I had only read a couple of pages. "Good."

"Let's have a drink."

In the bar we sat in semidarkness slowly sipping red wine. I watched his face as he talked about some of his classes at university. His skin was clear and he had tiny laugh lines around his eyes.

"I can't wait for us to be in school together next year." He reached across the table and wrapped his long fingers around mine. "Let's go. We've got to get up early tomorrow and I'm beat."

When Brian closed the door behind us, I felt better. I was warm and relaxed from the wine. I walked over to the window and opened the shutters.

Outside the snow was falling lightly. Brian came up

behind me and wrapped his arms around my waist, pulling me to him. I could feel his body pressing against mine.

He bent to kiss the top of my head.

"It's so beautiful," I whispered into the night as we watched the snow.

"Yes," he said softly. "Beautiful." His kisses sent a wild tingling sensation through me. He turned me so I was facing him. We held each other tightly.

Catching my breath, I pushed myself away.

"I get the bathroom first. You get to choose beds." My voice was shaky.

He must think I'm acting like a child. What am I doing here? Except it's exactly where I want to be.

I closed the bathroom door and locked it.

Back in the room Brian was sitting up in bed. His bare chest startled me even though I'd seen it a million times. I guess boys didn't wear pajamas, or at least if they did, maybe only the bottoms. I silently hoped he was wearing something.

I picked up my book and slipped into the second bed.

Brian got out of bed.

"My turn," he said. I didn't dare look anywhere but at my novel.

I didn't read. I listened to the sound of him brushing his teeth. I smiled to myself. It was as if we were married.

I heard him open the door to come back and I immediately looked down at my book. But I sensed that something was funny and had to look up.

He had pulled his shorts high up to his chest so they were pulling up in his groin and he was walking like a clown. Pretending to trip, he fell forward. I burst out laughing.

He picked himself up and came over to the side of the bed. Taking my book away, he laid it on the bedside table. We held each other and our hearts beat wildly.

"Sal," he breathed, "I want you."

"Oh, Brian."

"Do you?"

My heart was pounding. Yes. I hesitated.

In a faint breath I whispered, "No. Not yet. I'm not ready."

Brian looked into my eyes. Then he kissed them tenderly.

"That's all right, love. We've got lots of time." I felt his body relax. He kissed my nose, my cheeks, my lips. Together we breathed deeply.

I couldn't believe it. We had come so close.

10

THE ICY WIND SWEPT across the snow, throwing a slight spray into our faces. My chin and nose were tucked into my turtleneck and my ski hat was pulled down, leaving a small slit for my eyes. I could feel the snow clinging to my lashes.

I tried to lean closer to Brian. The chairlift was swaying as it slowly moved up the slope of the mountain.

Brian looked over at me, his eyes twinkling. "Well, at least it's not snowing."

"Great," I said, but through the layers of wool all that came out was a muffled grunt.

"And look at that glorious fresh snow. We'll be the first ones to make tracks down the Blue."

"I'd rather be in my nice warm bed."

Brian reached around my shoulders and pulled me closer. I could hardly feel him through all my clothing.

"Now, why didn't you mention that earlier?"

"How can we be doing this to ourselves and think it's fun? We're nuts. And you—you're the biggest nut of all because you really do think this is fun."

"Look up at the top tower. When we get there we're going to pop through the clouds into glorious sunshine."

"Always the total optimist."

There was little sunshine at the top, but once I was off the chair I felt warmer. We checked our bindings and slipped our poles over our mitts. It was incredibly quiet. Brian always loved to be first. First up, first at breakfast, first on the chairlift and first down the Blue Chair.

It took me a minute to loosen up and get the rhythm, but soon I was caught up in the magic. My turns were smooth and close as I glided through the fresh powder.

I could see Brian ahead. He was a much better skier than I was, much stronger and faster, but he never let himself get too far ahead of me. Since I had known him my skiing had improved tremendously. At first it was a real effort to keep up with him. But I didn't want to be left on the bunny hill so I learned quickly. Now it was almost easy.

It felt good, and I was proud to be his partner.

At the bottom, Brian looked back up the hill and admired his tracks.

"Boy, aren't they beauties? I wonder how long they'll last?"

We were able to make four good runs before the hill began to get crowded. There were many tracks now and it was difficult to pick ours out from the others.

"It looks as if it's time to push on. Are you ready to head over to the bowl?" Brian asked.

"Ready," I answered as I looked behind me to catch the chair.

When we reached the top of the lift we skied to a T-bar that took us up into the bowl. On a clear day this was my favorite spot on the whole mountain. For miles and miles all you could see was blue sky and sparkling white mountaintops. The place seemed like the top of the world.

Today, however, there was no blue sky and you couldn't see farther than the bowl itself. There was one advantage, though. There were very few skiers.

We dug our poles in and pushed off for a quick start. Gaining speed, we skied fast and hard. I followed Brian. He followed me. We crisscrossed paths down and around the moguls. Stopping every now and then to catch our breath, we kissed.

At noon we decided to buy some sandwiches and hike up to the peak behind the main runs. Then afterward we would ski down through the untouched powder.

When we were almost at the top, Brian looked back at me.

"Come on, Sal, we're almost there."

I was too exhausted to answer but I grinned.

Once I reached Brian he pushed me and I collapsed into the snow. He fell down beside me and held me close to him. He poked his icy nose into my cheek and I screamed. His lips were blue, but when we kissed I felt on fire.

There were only the two of us. This was the nearest place to heaven. We looked in each other's eyes and our hearts pounded.

Finally he released me and I spoke. "I'm so hot."

"I'll say. I think I'd better cool you off." Brian reached for some soft snow.

"No," I squealed as he threw a mittful of snow in my face.

Before I knew it the day had passed and we were making our last run down the mountain. It was long and easy — a perfect ending to a perfect day.

We were strapping our skis to the car in the parking lot when we heard familiar voices.

"Where have you two been all day? We've skied every run on this mountain looking for you."

"Joan, Barry!" I exclaimed. "What are you doing here?"

"Great luck," said Barry, beaming from ear to ear. "There was a small fire in the kitchen last night so Harry had to close down the restaurant for the weekend. And poor Joan here wasn't well enough to go into the store today. I thought a nice day in the fresh air would be the best cure for her." Barry winked at Joan. "How are you feeling, my dear?"

Joan raised her mitt to her forehead. "A little faint. I'm afraid I need a drink."

"Perfect! Let's head into the Après," Brian suggested.

As we finished with our skis I looked across the top of the car at Brian.

Last night I had wanted Joan and Barry to be here, but now I felt disappointed. The question of what would happen tonight had filled me with suspense all day. Now I felt let down.

There was no sign on Brian's face that he felt the same. That made me feel even worse. He probably hadn't thought about it all day. Or maybe after last night, he didn't want to be alone with me.

"There goes our private suite," I said, trying to make it sound light.

Brian came around the car, grabbed my hands and headed toward the bar.

"You'll just have to stifle your screams of joy as I ravish you in silence."

When he tried to tickle me I ran up the steps. He caught me at the top and kissed me. I felt the passion that had been building up inside me all day.

"I love you, Super Skier," I said.

Brian kissed the tip of my nose. We turned and went into the building arm in arm.

11

WE AWOKE THE NEXT morning to freezing rain. The mountain had been closed. It was below zero and there was a twenty-mile-per-hour wind. Visibility was nil. Even if we could have stood the bitter winds, we wouldn't have been able to see past the tips of our skis.

In the cafeteria I poked at runny scrambled eggs while the others tried to make jokes.

"What shall we do all morning?" Barry asked, looking at his watch. "There's no way I can go back to bed. And there's no point driving down the mountain until the traffic lessens."

"Why don't you call the Bakers?" I suggested. "They're probably hanging around for the day and maybe some of their company has gone."

"It's only eight o'clock," sighed Joan. "They'll have all gone back to bed. We can't phone yet."

"You're right," said Brian. "Let's pack up and drive to Green Meadows first to have a look at the new development. I wouldn't mind checking out how much those lots are going for."

"Since when do you have any money to buy a lot?" Barry looked suspicious.

"I don't, but they aren't going to get any cheaper." He winked at me and I felt my heart beating faster. "A man has to think about his future."

There were still a dozen people at the Bakers' when we arrived. Marisa greeted us at the door.

"I'm so glad you're here. Mother is making a huge pot of chili for lunch and we'd love it if you could stay."

The Bakers' doors were always open to everyone. Marisa and her two brothers had been brought up on skis, and the whole family spent almost every weekend at their cabin.

We sat at the long wooden table and stuffed our faces with chili. Mrs. Baker was a great cook and liked to see us devouring her food. The boys certainly weren't letting her down.

Brian began to talk about the prices of the lots we had just seen. Mr. Baker asked him more and more questions. At first the conversation was interesting, but soon they were into heavy finance and the increasing value of land.

I glanced down at my wrist to check the time. My watch was missing.

"Oh, no! I left my watch at the lodge." I jumped up.

"That's okay, Sal," Brian said. "We'll go back and pick it up on the way home."

"No. Listen. I've had enough of this high finance anyway. I know exactly where I left it. I'll just go back and get it quickly. You and Mr. Baker are still talking."

Joan jumped up, too. "I'll come with you." She looked at the stack of dishes. "Or maybe I'd better stay here and help with the dishes. That way we'll be ready to go when you get back. Do you mind going alone?"

"No. I'll be back before you finish."

Brian threw me the keys. "Drive carefully." I was out the door before anyone could say more.

The roads were icy and it was snowing lightly. I reached the lodge without any problems and quickly explained to the man at the desk what had happened. He let me into our room and there was my watch lying on the counter in the bathroom. I slipped it onto my wrist, thanked him and went out.

It was snowing more heavily. The road was mostly downhill to the Bakers', and I had to keep putting on the brakes to keep from picking up too much speed. My fingers were wrapped tightly around the steering wheel, my fingernails digging into my palms. I felt my shoulders hunch up, tight with tension as I tried to see through the snow. The wipers barely cleared the windshield before it was covered again.

I breathed in deeply, trying to stay calm.

Suddenly the car lurched forward as the wheels locked on a sheet of ice. I jammed my foot on the brakes. The MG fishtailed hard to the left and then to the right.

"Steer into the turn, into the turn." I could hear

Brian's voice echoing in my head. My heart was pounding so loudly I couldn't think.

The car was drifting down the hill toward a gray barrier where the road made a sharp turn. I turned the wheel hard. The car came around fast and swerved to the left. I turned hard to the right.

"Brian…" I screamed. The road slipped sideways. Steel shattered steel.

I lay still. A rock pierced my ear. I couldn't move my head. It was as though my head were nailed to the rock. The pain throbbed.

"Brian," I whimpered. "I can't move. Help me get up. Please, somebody help me."

I'm buried in snow, I thought. Nothing hurts except my ear. Why can't I move my head? I've got to get off this rock.

I listened but couldn't hear anything except a roar in my ear.

Finally, a car door slammed, a car engine roared. Down here, I tried to cry out. Please, down here.

There was a man beside me. I could only see his feet, then his knees as he knelt down.

"It's okay. We're here. There'll be help soon."

"Please, help me get up. Get this snow off me. I can't move."

"Take it easy," he said gently. "Don't try to move. Just lie still." The man took off his ski jacket and laid it across my shoulders.

"Please, my ear, it hurts so much," I whimpered.

I closed my eyes and pressed them tightly. It didn't help. The blackness whirled around in my head. I felt as if I were spinning, as if I were going to be flung even farther into the darkness. I struggled to open my eyes.

From somewhere far away a voice was repeating, "Your name, what is your name?"

"Sally," I moaned into the spinning blackness. "Please make it stop spinning."

"Sally, open your eyes. Stay awake. Open your eyes," the voice commanded.

Light filtered into the darkness. Everything was blurred. There was something in front of me. It was the man kneeling by my head in the snow. He was leaning over me. I felt him touch the top of my head. He slipped his ski hat, soft and wet, beneath it. A stabbing pain pierced my neck. My head seemed so heavy, as though a massive weight was pushing it down.

"Where are you staying?" the man asked. "Are you with friends?"

I tried to look up into his face. "Brian. I want Brian."

"Where is Brian?"

"Bakers' cabin." I struggled for the words. "End of Cedar Lane."

"Now lie still. Don't close your eyes. I'm going to send someone for Brian and be right back."

Brian would make me better. He would get me out from under this snow.

I heard a car stop, and voices. Then the car left.

The car.

In a few moments the man was back kneeling in front of me.

"Hi, you all right?" he asked, pulling his jacket close around my shoulders.

"The car," I blurted out. "Where is the car?"

"It's fine. Don't worry, everything will be fine. My name is Joe. I'll stay with you until Brian comes."

He asked me all kinds of questions to keep me talking. I can't remember how long I lay there, but it seemed like forever.

When the ambulance and a couple of police cars arrived I was very frightened. The attendants lifted me up very gently, keeping me perfectly stiff as though I were frozen in a block of ice, and placed me on a stretcher. I realized there was nothing on top of me. I couldn't understand why it felt as if I was lying under something heavy. What was wrong with me? I wanted Brian.

I heard a great commotion outside the ambulance. There was a lot of yelling. I felt lost, as if I had already died. I stared at the ceiling of the ambulance. I tried to move my head, but they had wrapped an ice pack around my neck and secured my head in a fixed position with pillows. I couldn't move my arms.

Why am I tied so tightly to this stretcher? I want to move my arms. Please, let me move.

The door flung open and a gust of icy air filled the

van. Brian leaped in and was beside me. He knelt by my head and touched my face. My eyes filled with tears and he stroked them off.

"Brian," I whimpered, "they've tied me down. I can't move. Please hold me. Let me touch you."

Brian leaned over and, barely touching me, he kissed me gently. Love rushed through me, holding me, giving me comfort.

He swallowed hard and spoke very softly, "Honey, you mustn't try to move. You've hurt your neck and you must keep it very, very still."

"I'm so glad you're here. Touch me. I've got to feel you."

Brian stroked my cheek with his finger. His breath was warm on my face.

"It's okay, baby. Everything is going to be okay. We'll have you fixed up in no time."

I felt the ambulance jerk as we started to move. I was barely aware of the second attendant who sat behind Brian watching me quietly.

"Where are Joan and Barry?" I asked.

"They've gone ahead. They'll meet us at the hospital."

"Boy, I've sure ruined a good weekend," I said, feeling tears well up inside me.

"You've done no such thing." He held me with his eyes. I felt a strength I had never known before. "Has anyone ever told you that you're beautiful?"

His smile was contagious. "No, not unless they wanted something."

"You'd better not be difficult, young lady," Brian said and kissed the end of my nose. "You're not in any position to resist."

"How about saving it for a little later so that I can enjoy it, too?"

"That's a deal," he said and kissed my nose again.

Somehow, just then, I thought everything was going to be all right.

12

I STARED UP AT the faces around me. Aware of people moving briskly, I lay on my back and focused on a gentle face. Warm brown eyes smiled at me as the woman brushed the hair out of my eyes like a mother watching over her sick child. In a soft, low voice she told me what she and the other nurses were doing.

"We're going to remove these wet clothes. First, your jacket." She leaned over me and, with her hands spread, held my head as in a vise.

"Oh," I screamed. "My ear."

"I'm sorry," she said, easing her hand down without lessening her grip. "We'll fix that up soon."

She held me still while the others removed my clothing without moving me.

"I'm afraid we'll have to cut your shirt. We can't take it over your head."

I didn't care about my shirt. I didn't care about anything except getting fixed up. I was freezing and wanted to wrap my arms in front of me to keep warm.

I heard the clip of the scissors and waited to feel cold steel against my skin. It didn't come.

"Here's Dr. Wood." The nurse smiled at me. "You'll like him. He's a wonderful doctor."

"Hi, Sally," a tall, thin man in a white jacket said as he reached down and picked up my hand. "Can you squeeze my hand?"

His hands were cold and I could feel the pressure of his hand holding mine, but I couldn't move my fingers.

"They're numb," I said. He laid my hand down beside me and reached over for my other one.

My God! My arms weren't tied down at all. They were just lying limp at my sides.

"Why can't I move my arms?" Why do they feel so heavy? What have I done?

"Squeeze my hands," Dr. Wood directed me.

I held my breath and pushed with every ounce of energy I had left. Nothing.

The tears swelled in my eyes.

"What's the matter, doctor? Why am I so numb?" I searched his eyes, looking for some kind of sign. Was he worried? I couldn't tell.

"Now, Sally, I'm going to take a small pin and I want you to tell me when you can feel it." He moved toward the end of the bed.

"Can you feel that?"

"No."

"That?"

"No."

"That?"

"No." I felt like screaming.

He moved up my body asking the same question. When he got to my breastbone I felt a slight pinch.

"Yes. I feel it! I feel it!"

"Good." He smiled down at me reassuringly. I tried not to think.

The doctor picked up my arm again. He began pricking the ends of my fingers.

"Now, don't look at me. Can you feel that?"

"No."

"That?"

"No."

"What finger am I holding?"

"My thumb," I squealed out. "I can feel my thumb."

"Now?"

"My index finger."

"Now?"

I wasn't sure. It felt as if he was holding three of my fingers. I wanted to be right.

"My ring finger?"

He continued to move up my arm, asking the same question. Then he looked over at the nurse and nodded. She left my side.

The next thing I knew Dr. Wood was sitting on a stool and his face was right beside mine.

"I'm going to shave a little of your hair off, Sally. Just

a small corner here on the side of your head. Then I have to drill a little hole in order to hook you up to traction. It shouldn't hurt, but the drill will make a noise. Try to relax. It won't take very long."

I heard the words and I knew what they meant but they seemed to float around in my head. I closed my eyes and felt as though I was drifting away, leaving my body. Behind me the roar of the drill vibrated into my skull but I was too far away to feel the pain.

When I woke up I was in a small space with white curtains drawn on both sides of me. Now not only was my body tied down, but my head was weighted down, pressing into the bed.

I tried to see what they had done to me but I couldn't turn sideways.

The pins they had stuck into my head frightened me. Looking up, I could see what looked like the top of a pulley system with two steel ropes hanging down behind my head. I knew that somehow the whole thing was attached to me.

Now I was really afraid.

Blankets lay across my chest and I could see that I was wearing a pink hospital gown. It looked like a plain cotton smock that had been put on backwards. I was desperately cold and longed to pull the covers up to my neck.

The nurse suddenly appeared inside my curtain.

"Hi, my name is Rosey. How are you feeling?"

I looked up at her.

"Feeling? I'm not feeling much of anything. But I'm tied down, freezing, and I have this ache in my head."

She smiled and I saw real compassion in her light brown eyes.

"Here, let me get you a nice warm blanket." She turned away and was back in a minute. She threw the blanket over me, pulled it up and tucked it under my chin.

"There, is that a little better?"

The blanket felt as though it had been in a toasting oven, and I was sharing a bit of the oven's warmth.

"Thank you," was all I could say.

She began to speak gently.

"You are in the Intensive Care Unit at City Hospital. You are in good hands and we will do everything to make you as comfortable as possible." She paused. "Can you tell me your name?"

Frowning, I answered, "Sally."

"Do you know where you are?"

Still frowning. "City Hospital. Intensive Care. You just told me."

"How old are you?"

"Eighteen. What is this?"

"We just want to make sure you are aware." Her tone was sweet and I knew I shouldn't be angry, but my frustration made me snap.

"Then tell me what's going on. What's happened? Where's Brian?"

"The doctor will talk to you in a little while." She

pulled out a thermometer and flicked it with her wrist. "Now I must take your temperature and your blood pressure," she said, sticking the thin glass tube under my tongue. She reached under the cover and pulled my arm out into the cold air. She wrapped a black band around my arm and fastened it. She blew the band up until it was tight on my arm. She put a stethoscope in her ears and listened to my pulse as the air released.

When she pulled the band off, the ripping of the Velcro made me wince.

Leaving the thermometer in my mouth, she picked up my wrist and felt my pulse. She carefully replaced my arm at my side under the covers.

Rosey pulled the thermometer out of my mouth.

"Where's Brian?" I repeated.

"He's waiting outside."

"Can I see him now?"

"Dr. Wood is coming to see you first. If he says it's all right, then Brian may come in."

The mere suggestion that I might not be allowed to see Brian caused a huge lump to rise in my throat and tears to fill my eyes.

"You must let Brian in," I whimpered. "I have to see him."

"I'm sure he'll be able to," Rosey said, wiping a tear from my cheek. "Please don't upset yourself. Dr. Wood will be here soon. Try and relax. Everything will be all right."

I realized my head, my neck, my shoulders — the only

parts of my body that I could feel — were strained and tense. I took a deep breath and swallowed hard. I didn't want to cry.

Why was this happening to me? I couldn't believe it, and yet I knew it wasn't a dream. I knew it was real.

Dr. Wood came from behind the curtain. He was followed by the head nurse, I knew from her badge. He handed his clipboard to the nurse, reached under the blanket and picked up my hand. He had long white teeth that emphasized his long face and high cheekbones.

I looked from his balding head into the cold hazel eyes. It looked as though he had seen a lot of pain, and I was just another sad case.

"Where did you get the nice tan? You're the picture of perfect health."

"Skiing," I said quietly, suddenly afraid to say more.

"Can you squeeze my hand?"

I tried. He put that hand back under the covers and reached for the other one.

"How about your left? Can you squeeze it?"

"No."

He gently placed it back and pulled the covers up to my neck. He took the clipboard from the nurse and wrote a few things down.

I waited quietly, watching his eyes, pleading with them to tell me that everything was going to be all right. They rose from the board and met mine. We stared at each other for a few seconds.

"Sally, you've injured your neck. It's going to be a long, hard struggle, but you look like a pretty determined young lady."

"Am I going to be all right?" I blurted.

"It's too soon to tell exactly what damage has been done. Your spinal cord is swollen and we have to wait until the swelling goes down. But," his attempt to smile was weak, "you're going to be fine. Now, this bed that you're lying in is called a Stryker frame. You have weights attached to your head which are pulling the vertebrae back into position. Every two hours you have to be turned over in order to keep the tension on your spine even. The nurses will tell you how it works. If you need anything they will help you."

"Can I see Brian now?"

"You shouldn't have too many visitors yet."

"Please," I begged.

"All right." He turned to the nurse. "Only for a short visit."

I've often tried to remember exactly what happened when Brian saw me for the first time. I can only remember him being there, sitting close to me at the head of the bed, holding my hand and playing with my useless fingers. Tears rolled from the corners of my eyes, down across my temples and into my ears before reaching the bed sheets.

"I'm sorry, sir." Rosey's words cut into our world. "We have to turn Sally now. I'm afraid you'll have to leave."

Brian's eyes had not left mine. He saw my sudden fear. Slowly he turned sideways and looked up at Rosey.

"I'm going to stay until she's turned."

It was not a question. Turning back to me he squeezed my hand and leaned to kiss my cheek.

"I'll be right here."

His breath was warm against my skin. I wanted to grab him. He stepped back to let the orderlies near and then he went to the end of the bed where I could see him.

I tried to hold onto his eyes.

Two orderlies laid a canvas frame, with an oval hole for my face, on top of me. They secured it tightly with straps. Rosey held the weights attached to the "ice tong" calipers and my head, while the orderlies flipped me over.

I was suddenly face down, staring at a small area of floor below me. They undid the straps and took the bottom — now the top — frame off me. The oval for my face was padded but I could feel it biting into my forehead and chin. All I could see was white legs and shoes.

"Brian," I cried into the floor. I recognized the brown loafers and the bottom of his cords as he came around to the top of this horrible contraption that I was imprisoned in. I saw his knees and then realized that he was getting down on the floor. He slid under the frame.

On his back he was close to me once more.

"Brian, here," he saluted, "under your command."

We both laughed weakly.

"I have to go now, Sal. The doctor says you must get some rest. I've called your parents and they'll be here as soon as they can. I'll be right here and will come back as soon as they let me." He raised his finger up to my face and brushed my cheek. "I love you." He formed a kiss with his mouth and gently touched the end of my nose with his finger. I watched his feet disappear.

My pulse beat quickly, throbbing high in my forehead as it pressed against the canvas. I tried to hold back my tears but they dripped to the floor. I closed my eyes hard.

"Please, dear Lord, please help me to recover. I know it seems as if I only come to you when I'm in trouble, but please help me to be strong. I know I can do it but I need your help. I promise I'll be good, I'll be the best person in the whole world, but please get me out of this mess," I sobbed.

"Sally." Already Rosey's voice was familiar to me. It was as if I had been there for days and yet it had only been several hours. "Sally, you mustn't cry. Everything is going to be fine. Here, let me dry your face." I opened my eyes to her red face as she peered under the Stryker frame. She held a tissue up to my eyes. "Here, can you blow your nose?"

I took a breath and tried to blow.

"I can't," I blubbered. "I can't even blow my nose."

"There, there." She stood up and rubbed my shoulder. It was wonderful to feel something. At least somewhere I could feel someone touching me. She must have stood there for a while as I drifted off into exhausted sleep.

I awoke to the shuffle of people around me. From the pain in my forehead and chin I thought the edges of the oval face hole must have cut into me. Thank God they were going to turn me.

I held my breath as the weight of the top frame made the pain unbearable.

"Hurry," I cried out. "For God's sake, hurry."

A deep voice counted, "One, two, three."

My stomach flew into my throat and I spun into blackness. I choked and threw up, only to choke again on my own vomit. Hands flew as they removed the top frame. A different nurse held a wet towel up to my mouth. Gently she turned my head sideways. I tried to spit out the vile taste in my mouth, but it just dribbled down my face.

Now I knew this nightmare was for real.

God, let me die, I begged silently. Let me die.

"You'll feel better in a minute," the nurse whispered. She wiped the cold cloth around my face.

"It's cold," I complained, "and I'm freezing. Where's Rosey?"

"Rose has gone off shift. I'm Marilyn. I'll get you a warm cloth and a blanket."

She disappeared for a minute, leaving me to breathe in my own stench. I lay there afraid to move, afraid to breathe, praying I would die.

Marilyn returned instantly with a pile of fresh things.

"Where's my mother and father?" I demanded. "Why hasn't my mother been here?"

"They're waiting outside. As soon as we clean you up you can see them."

"How long have they been here?"

"About an hour."

"Why haven't they come in?"

"They have, but you were asleep."

"I want my parents."

I lay pinned to the bed, staring at the ceiling as I strained to hear my parents. I heard footsteps and tried to lift my head.

Suddenly my father was standing beside me. He leaned down to kiss me as tears filled my eyes.

"Daddy," I choked out. "I've broken my neck."

"It's all right, honey. Everything is going to be all right." He kissed me again and stroked my wet cheeks.

"Don't people die…"

He quickly put his finger on my lips to stop me.

"Ssh! No one is going to let my baby die. You are going to be just fine." He sat down beside the bed and we held each other with our eyes.

When I was young, whenever I hurt myself I would sit on Dad's knee and he would hold me close and rock me. I imagined I was there in his lap.

After a few moments I whispered, "Where's Mom?"

"They will only allow one visitor in at a time. House

rules," he said, shrugging. His face was so familiar and my heart leaped out to him. He leaned down to kiss me again as tears refilled my eyes.

"I wanted to see you first," he said softly.

Dad sat quietly for a few moments. When he recovered, he began talking.

"We've had a long talk with the doctors. I told them I want the very best care for my little girl. I have been assured there isn't a finer doctor than Dr. Wood."

"He seems nice." I started to nod my head and then stopped as the tongs cut into me.

"Honey, are you in very much pain?"

"No, Dad. I'm just scared. I feel numb all over."

"Don't be afraid. You're going to be fine." He kissed me again. "I love you, Sally."

"I love you too, Daddy."

"Your mother is waiting. I must let her see you. We're only allowed a short visit tonight, but we'll be here first thing in the morning. Good night, honey."

13

"Hi, darling," Mother sang out cheerfully. I heard her greetings to the nurses and then her familiar walk before she came into view. She was wearing the usual sterile pink gown over her brown woolen suit.

I had never cared much for that suit before, but now it was wonderful to see something other than hospital garb, even though it was mostly covered by the gown.

For a minute I wondered if I would ever wear normal clothes again.

She placed a large paper bag on the bedside table.

"How's my girl today?"

"Fine," I answered. "Dr. Wood said that my bones have pulled back into place sooner than he expected, that the X-rays have been good."

"That's wonderful! I know you're going to be out of that thing in no time. Now, let's see what's for lunch today." She reached over and pulled the stainless-steel warmer off the tray. "Ah, shepherd's pie. It looks good."

"I wish you were right," I said, ignoring the food, "but

he says it'll take a long time to heal. There's one thing I've got and that's time. Just as long as I get well, I can wait."

I tried not to watch my mother's eyes as she fed me lunch. I hated being fed just as I hated someone else washing my face and cleaning my teeth. By making light conversation she tried not to show how she felt, but her pain radiated from her body and her blue eyes were dull and often misty.

Still, it was much nicer being fed by her than by one of the nurses, who were usually in a hurry and sometimes fed two patients at once. Many times when it got around to my turn the food was cold and unappetizing.

My bed flips were organized so that I was always on my back at meal times. I couldn't imagine having to eat on my stomach staring at the floor.

"Brian called this morning to say he would be a little late tonight but that he would be in time for dinner. He has to take the car in, but it shouldn't take very long."

The mention of Brian's car sent a twang of guilt through me. He had saved so long to buy the MG. I had destroyed his pride and joy.

Mother saw the look on my face.

"It won't be more than thirty minutes. I'll stay a little longer if you like."

"It's not that, Mom. It's just that I feel so bad about the car."

"The car! Don't be silly. All that Brian cares about is that you get better."

"Mom, what have I done? I'm causing everyone so much pain. What if I don't get better? What if I never walk again? I'll have to spend the rest of my life in bed or in a wheelchair." I couldn't hold back the tears as they rolled down my face.

"You mustn't think about it, Sally," she said, wiping my tears first, and then hers. "You're going to get better and that's all there is to it. We must have faith. And don't you worry about the rest of us. We're all fine. Just get yourself better. No matter what happens we'll all be here because we love you. You must never forget that."

"I know, Mom, and I love you. I just want to get out of this bed so badly."

"Oh, honey, I know." She suddenly changed her mood. "Listen. I have some great news. Charlie's coming home."

My stomach jumped. "When?"

"In two weeks. I wanted to surprise you, but I knew how happy you'd be."

"I thought he couldn't come home until he'd finished his exams."

"He's been trying to come ever since the accident. I don't think he can concentrate on his studies until he sees you."

"I don't want him to see me like this. If anything puts him off his studies, this will."

"Don't be silly," she said quickly. "We all need to be together. It will be wonderful to have him home, even if it is only for a few days."

At exactly one o'clock, Rosey and two orderlies interrupted our conversation.

"Are you ready to be flipped?" Rosey asked cheerfully.

"What if I said no?" I grumbled.

"It wouldn't do you any good," she smiled and then reached for the weights above my head.

Rosey had taken a special interest in me in the two weeks since I arrived. She knew I was always cold so she would slip a warm blanket out of the warmer and put it over me, as she did now. I was always glad when I was assigned to her for the day. Even when she wasn't my nurse she would come to visit whenever she had a spare minute.

When I had been turned over, Mother dove into her brown paper bag. Her hand rustled about as she pulled things out and laid them on the table.

"I brought you a new toothbrush, a brush so that we could get some of those tangles out of your hair, and a couple of new nighties." She spread two short nighties on the floor beneath my bed.

The flannel looked warm and cozy, a far cry from the horrible hospital gowns I had been wearing.

"I cut them up the back so that the nurses could get them on." She turned them over. I watched the movements of her fingers, so easy and natural. "See, I put a little tie here. They don't have any decent hospital nighties in the stores, so I made my own."

"Thanks, Mom. They're great." I tried to sound

pleased and I was, except for a faint nagging somewhere deep that made me wonder if from now on my life was going to be a series of adaptations.

"And look." She stuck something shiny under the bed. "Ta-da! A mirror." She placed a large round shaving mirror on the floor. I heard her ripping tape from a roll as I stared down at myself.

My face was the same. Nothing had changed except my skin was red and chafed where the oval pressed into me.

It really was me.

"There," Mother said as she picked up the mirror and taped it to the leg of the bed. "Now you'll be able to see what's going on around you. Can you see yourself?"

"I don't want to see myself."

"Oh, well then." She moved it and I saw her smile. "Can you see me?"

"Yes, Mom," I said quietly, not wanting to cry.

She moved out of view and I heard her rustling in the bag again. "If you'd like, I could brush your hair. Maybe if I put it in a braid on top of your head it wouldn't get so tangled."

"Fine."

Taking one clump at a time, she gently began to pull at the knots.

In the afternoons I had more free time than in the mornings, which were often busy. First there was breakfast, then my bed bath and personal care, and the changing of sheets. There were X-rays to be taken. The machines had to be brought to me as I couldn't be moved to the X-ray department. Every day I had blood tests. A physiotherapist came twice each day, once in the morning and once in the afternoon, to exercise my hands, arms and legs.

I was always anxious for my visit with Dr. Wood each morning. He said it would take time for any return of movement or feeling, but it had been two weeks. Two weeks of being strapped down and turned like a pig on a spit.

Well, my life wasn't over yet.

The first thing I tried to do each morning was wiggle my toes. I would make the nurses come and look. I couldn't see them myself.

"Are they moving? Are they moving?" I begged. "It feels as if they're moving."

Each morning they shook their heads. When the doctor held my hand I pressed and pressed but nothing happened. As he moved the pin up my body each day I closed my eyes and prayed, "Please, let me feel, let me feel."

Sometimes Dr. Wood would come around with other doctors, students or interns. I knew they didn't mean to, but they would surround the bed and talk over me as though I had no thoughts or feelings.

"She has a fracture of the body of C six and seven with serious displacement. It appears to be a complete lesion and she has no sensation from the nipple line down. At present there are no reflexes evident in her legs. She has a neurogenic bladder and bowel... She has developed the organism *Pseudomonas aeruginosa* which is sensitive to gentamicin and resistant to everything else."

I wanted to scream at them. "Talk to me. Tell me what you're saying. What does it mean? Will I walk?"

They had no answers, just a lot of smiles and pats. My thread of hope was fading fast.

It was the physiotherapist who finally told me the truth. I watched Sara impatiently as she slowly bent and stretched each finger to prevent them from tightening and curling. I looked at the mousy brown hair that clung to the side of her head in tight curls and wondered if she was as boring as she looked. I figured she must live in a one-bedroom apartment — the older kind in a two-story building, with a Siamese cat.

"When do you think my hands will come back?" I asked.

Her face was flat and had no color. She moved her eyes, a sterile pale blue, from my fingers to my eyes without a flicker of emotion.

"Oh, I don't think they will."

"What?" I stammered. "The doctor said they might."

"He may have said there was a chance, but from the look of your X-rays, I'd say there wasn't much chance at all."

My throat seized up.

"And my legs? What about my legs? I suppose you think I'll never walk again?" I tried to pull my hand from hers but of course I couldn't.

She continued with the exercises. "Sally, there are lots of people who live perfectly normal lives in a wheelchair and many are worse off than you. You should be thankful that you're alive."

I wanted to scream at her but the words came out cracked and muffled.

"What can I do without my hands? Look at me. What can I do?" My throat and chest heaved with pain as I tried to control my tears.

Her voice was softer but matter-of-fact.

"You'll be surprised at the things you'll be able to do. You have wrist movement and your arms will get stronger. It will take time but you'll learn to do most things for yourself, with the aid of a few gadgets."

"No!" I shouted. "I won't listen to you. What can you know?"

I turned my head away from her as far as I could. A sharp pain cut across my skull.

Sara got up.

"I'll see you tomorrow," she said and left.

I don't want you, I thought angrily. I hate you.

I closed my eyes tightly and concentrated on moving my toes.

Come on, move. Move. I could feel where they were. They felt as if I could move them. My whole body felt the same from the inside except for the numbness. I could feel my toes, my legs, my stomach. Except sometimes I would think my legs were in one position and then I would see that they weren't that way at all.

I couldn't understand how I could feel on the inside and not on the outside. Sara had told me that the sensation was common. When someone lost an arm or a leg they still had the feeling that it was there.

I kept checking, looking and feeling the parts of me I could reach to make sure I was still there. Because it felt as if I were moving my toes, I kept on trying. Sara had to be wrong.

Please, God, let her be wrong. I've got to get better.

Suddenly I was aware of someone near me. I opened my eyes to see Brian watching me.

"Hi, honey, I didn't want to wake you."

"I wasn't asleep," I said, so glad to see him. "Oh, Brian, she said I'd never walk again. She said my hands wouldn't come back." I cried, the tears rolling freely down my cheeks.

He reached his arm across me and held onto my shoulder. Putting his face next to mine, he held me as well as he could.

"Honey, honey, who said that to you?"

"Sara."

"Sally," Brian raised his head and kissed my wet face, "we mustn't let people like Sara get to us. She doesn't know. Nobody does."

"Then why would she say it?"

"Some people are born pessimists. They like to think the worst. Then, if things get better, they're pleasantly surprised. I guess she's seen a lot of people who haven't recovered."

"I hate her. You know, she didn't even care."

Brian sat up straight. "Forget about Sara. I'm not going to stop praying, and I don't expect you to."

We were both quiet for a few minutes. Brian, of course, was right. We mustn't give up hope. But she seemed so sure. Why hadn't Dr. Wood said anything? He'd seen the X-rays.

I felt so lost. I wanted to know the answers, but I was afraid of what they might be.

"I brought you a note from Joan. She thinks it's most unfair that she's not allowed to visit." He reached under his pink gown and pulled out an envelope. "Would you like me to read it to you?"

"Yes, please." I was sad that Joan and Barry couldn't visit, but I was grateful that they let Brian come. After all, he wasn't really part of the family. I was also grateful that they allowed him to stay for longer than the regulated five minutes.

I guess they knew I wouldn't make it without him.

14

THE DAY I WAS moved from the Intensive Care Unit was the last day I had any hope. I had been out of the Stryker frame for a week and it was absolute heaven not to be in that canvas sandwich. I was in a normal hospital bed but still had weights hanging from my head. Dr. Wood had told me that the bones in my neck were nicely in place and that he didn't think it would be necessary to fuse the vertebrae in an operation.

I was relieved, as I felt that cutting into my spine might mean permanent damage with no chance of recovery.

All the nurses crowded the door to say goodbye as they wheeled me out. Rosey came with me, carrying the weights while an orderly pushed me along to room 310.

It was exciting to be moved from my six-by-eight white-curtained space. My eyes strained to see everything. I wanted to slow down so that I wouldn't miss a face, a door, a station. I needed to know my surroundings.

The splash of light and color that flooded over me as my stretcher went through the door made me gasp. My eyes feasted on a large window with red and orange checkered curtains. Outside I could see blue sky and a building across the street.

There was still a world out there after all.

Along the window ledge, on the dresser and on the bedside table were fifteen different arrangements of mums, carnations and daisies, and closest to my bed was a fabulous display of baby red roses. My eyes flew to Rosey's.

Her eyes twinkled.

"Brian?" I asked, and she nodded.

"Oh, how wonderful! Where did all the rest come from?"

"You weren't allowed to have flowers in ICU so we asked the florist to save them. I called them yesterday. Let's get you into your new bed and then I'll read you the cards."

With one quick movement orderlies slid me with a sheet from the stretcher to the bed. Rosey set up my weights, attached my catheter and urine bag to the side of the bed and covered me up with fresh blankets.

"I should have snuck you one last warm blanket. I'm afraid you're not going to be so spoiled down here," she smiled.

"I'll say not. There'll be no foolish pampering in this ward," a tall heavyset woman said. "We will look after her from now on, thank you," she added, trying to dismiss Rosey.

As she came closer to the bed a smell of stale smoke

drifted over me. Her hair was gray and frizzy and was held back from her face with a bobby pin. I looked at her yellowish-white uniform and cringed. There was a slop of food on her bosom.

"You can return to your own ward where I'm sure they need your expertise," she said in a husky voice.

"I'm on my break, Mrs. Holt, and I'm having a visit with Sally."

We watched as she moodily checked the weights and the bedding. She gave a disgusted look at my flowers and turned toward the door.

Over her shoulder she said gruffly, "Visiting hours are from four to eight," and left the room.

I looked at Rosey. "What will I do?"

"Don't worry about Mrs. Holt. She's just a harmless grump."

"I'm going to miss you so much."

"No, you won't, because I'll come to visit you every day."

"That will be fabulous. Will you bring Robert? I'd love to meet that handsome man of yours."

Rosey's eyes shifted to the window. I saw a look of sadness on her face that I had never seen before.

"Rosey, what's happened?"

"Robert and I broke up. He's going to New Zealand to do his internship."

"Oh," I moaned. "I'm sorry. Why don't you go with him?"

"Mrs. Langley is leaving ICU at the end of the month and I'll be the new head nurse. I've worked hard for this position and I don't want to give it up. I guess I don't love him as much as I thought…"

Neither one of us spoke. The only sound was street drilling from outside.

Rosey stood up and smiled. "Now, you make sure they turn you and remind them to put splints on your hands at night. If they don't your fingers will curl."

"I will. Thanks for fixing up the room. It's beautiful."

"Okay, kid. I'll see you later."

With that she turned and left me alone in my new surroundings.

How could Robert leave her? How could anybody leave her?

I glanced at my roses and pictured Brian.

I knew it would be just a matter of time before I felt her pain, before Brian realized he didn't love me.

Oh, please love me a little bit longer.

I looked from bouquet to bouquet thinking about the people who had sent me flowers. Surely I could get better with all those people praying for me.

Please, Brian, don't leave me yet.

Mother came as usual to feed me lunch. I was quiet as she did my hair and nails while we waited nervously for school to be over and my friends to come for the first time.

Joan and Barry were the first to arrive.

For a moment they stood out of sight at the bottom of the bed, afraid to come near. I swallowed hard. Tears were creeping into my eyes. I felt Joan fighting back tears, too, and I knew it was up to me to break the awkward silence.

"I'm so glad you're here," I said. "Come here where I can see you."

With that Joan rushed over and threw her arm across my chest. Our wet cheeks pressed together as we cried. Then, laughing, she stood up and made room for Barry to lean down and kiss my cheek.

That was always the hardest – the moment when someone came to see me for the first time. They never knew what their reaction was going to be and they were afraid of showing their grief. Of course, they didn't know what to expect and were tense from the anticipation. I learned that I had to make things right. I had to be cheerful and make jokes to put them at ease.

At first it wasn't too hard because I believed everything was going to be fine, that this was a temporary setback. However, as time passed, it became harder and harder to keep up the act.

Barry turned his back and looked out of the window.

"My, the lady even has a view." His voice was jovial, but I knew he had turned to hide tears.

"Yes, and look at all the glorious flowers. Ooh, who sent the roses?"

"Brian," I beamed. "He must have been really bad!"

"Boy, that's the thanks I get for being a nice guy."

"Brian," we said, relieved to see him.

"What a bunch of sad faces. This is supposed to be happy hour." With that he put his gym bag on a chair and unzipped it. Reaching in, he pulled out a bag of potato chips and threw them at Barry.

"*Servez les hors d'oeuvres, s'il vous plaît,* uh…while I pour the drinks," he added as we all laughed. He poured Coke into paper cups and passed them around. I watched as he put a straw in one and pulled a chair up to the side of the bed.

As he leaned in to kiss me he whispered, "Love you." Then he held the cup up for me to drink from while he went on talking. It seemed so natural, as though nothing was wrong.

I glanced at Mother and saw her smiling at Brian. I was glad she'd come to admire him. It made me feel closer to her. I only wished it hadn't cost me so much.

She caught my eyes on her.

"Dear, I must be off," she said as she patted my leg from the top of the bed covers. "I'll leave you young people alone."

"Don't go," said Brian. "The party's just begun."

"I must. I have to get supper for Dad. I'll see you tomorrow, Sally." She waved to everyone and left.

Barry and Joan relaxed and, as more and more friends came, it did turn into a happy hour.

Later, when everyone but Brian had left, I asked him, "Did you get the forms?"

"No, honey, there'll be lots of time for that. You were lucky to get a private room."

"Don't try to change the subject. The university is only accepting a limited number this year and I want to make sure I've got my application in on time. I wanted you to help me write a letter tonight. I didn't think it was too much to ask."

"That's right," he said, his voice rising. "You didn't think. Well, you'd better start thinking about others as well as yourself. I didn't have time to pick up your forms. I have a big paper due tomorrow. I skipped my classes just so I could finish it and not miss seeing you. I'm going to be up all night typing."

"Poor you," I moaned sarcastically.

"You're God damn right poor me." Brian poured himself a cup of Coke without offering me any. He drank it slowly, obviously trying to control his temper.

"Sally, it's going to take time for you to get back on your feet. Right now school's not important."

"Oh, I see. It's important for you but not for me." I could see the anger rising in him but I didn't care. "I don't want to miss a whole year. Even if I have to miss the exams, I can write the supplementary ones. But they have to know about me or I won't have a chance."

There was silence.

"Well, will you get them?"

"Jesus, Sally." He scrunched up the paper cup and threw it violently into the garbage can. "Why don't you just start concentrating a little harder on getting better? You should be thinking about getting up and out of here rather than about going to school."

"Start concentrating," I screamed back at him. "What do you think I do all day?"

Brian thrust his hands into his pockets and glared at me.

"I've got work to do," he said and walked out of the room.

The next evening Brian didn't come until well after supper. He slumped down into his chair without saying anything. His face was pale and his eyes were puffy.

"Brian," I started slowly. "I do concentrate. I stare at my toes for hours, begging them to move. I can't think about my toes all the time. I lie here for hours with nothing to do. I can't hold a book. There's nothing interesting on television. I have to think about something besides myself. You said I'd get better."

Brian sighed deeply. He didn't come close to me.

"Sally, don't you understand? It's going to take a long time." His voice was bitter. His words were slow and forced. "A long, hard time."

"Don't you think I've improved?"

"Yes," he said slowly as he leaned in nearer to me. "Yes, you have improved."

"Pull down the covers and let me show you something."

Brian raised his eyebrows.

"Only to my waist," I said flirtatiously.

My arms lay still at my sides. I strained to see my hand, but the weights held me down. I stared at the ceiling instead.

"Okay. Watch my right hand."

Very slowly I turned my wrist from one side to the other. By pulling up with my right shoulder, I rolled it little by little over my hip onto my stomach. I continued the wrist movement but now with the help of my bicep I pulled my hand up to my neck. By turning my head sideways I made a path to pull my hand onto my cheek.

Contact! Of course I couldn't move my fingers to scratch, but by moving my head back and forth and holding my wrist, I was able to rub my nose.

"Ta-da!" I exclaimed, using my mother's expression. "You are the first to witness me being able to scratch my nose."

"My God," Brian exclaimed. "All that for an itch?" He leaned in and kissed me.

"Do you know what it's like not being able to scratch your own nose?" I asked as I slid my hand back down to my side in the same way.

"Do you want to see something else?" I teased as Brian, knowing I was always cold, pulled the covers around my neck and tucked them under my chin.

"Go down to the bottom of the bed and watch my toes."

"Ah, a toe thrill," he teased as he headed for the end of the bed.

"Are you watching?"

"All ten."

I closed my eyes and concentrated the way I did every time I had a spare moment.

"Sally," he shrieked. "Sally, they're moving. That's wonderful. Do it again."

It was only my big toe. The rest of them felt as if they were embedded in cement.

"Sally, have you told Dr. Wood?" Brian asked.

"No, I'll show him tomorrow. The nurses think it's only a spasm."

"To hell with the nurses." He sat down. "I have a feeling things are looking up."

Just then the nurse came in. "Hi, I'm Corey, but everyone around here calls me Mother." She smiled and big dimples appeared in her cheeks. She looked from her watch to Brian and then to me. "I think we should get you ready to turn in. I've got a few medications to give out. Be back in ten minutes."

We both nodded, knowing she was politely dismissing Brian. When she left he kissed me lightly, our lips lingering gently, feeling for the thin thread of hope. I hated it when he had to leave. If only I could get up and go with him.

I lay in the darkness, my eyes wide open, staring at the small rosebuds clipped before their time. They were beautiful, but their beauty wouldn't last.

My toes, I thought. I was conscious of my routine effort to move my toes. First my right, then my left, with the same rhythm as if I were pedaling slowly up a steep hill.

I wanted an answer. How long is a long time?

The quiet bounced around the small room, making waves in the air that was warm and heavy with the fragrance of flowers. Out in the hall I could hear quick muffled steps and I pictured the white shoes that I knew so well. From a distance I could hear the nurses laughing.

I wondered who else was lying quietly alone, listening to them laugh.

15

"SALLY." DR. WOOD'S VOICE was low, almost a whisper, as though he didn't want me to hear what he was going to say.

I stared at his face. His dull greenish eyes looked defeated. His hollow cheeks were unshaven and he seemed tired.

"Tell me. I've been here four weeks and I want to know the truth."

I watched his thin lips move as he spoke.

"I can't say for sure exactly what recovery, if any, you will get. From what we have seen, I'm sorry, but it looks doubtful."

I felt myself float into a state of indifference. His words didn't make me feel sad or angry.

I heard myself say, "You mean, I'll never walk again?"

He paused and took a deep breath. "No, I'm afraid not."

"And my hands?"

"Very doubtful. Sally. I am not God. I cannot tell you exactly what will be. I can only tell you that from medical experience your chances of recovery are almost nil. I can, however, assure you that you will be able to live a full life. You will be amazed at the amount you will be able to do with your limited functions." I could see his hands clenched inside the pockets of his white jacket.

"What happens next?" I asked, feeling a cold cloud envelop me.

"You will have to stay in traction for two more weeks. Then, if we feel that your neck is stable, we will remove the weights, and you will wear a neck brace for a short while. There is an excellent rehabilitation center in the city where you will go when you are strong enough and when they have a bed available for you."

My head alone turned toward the window, away from him and his words. I had no thoughts or feelings. I was numb like the rest of my body. There was no direction, no life — nothing.

The day drifted into evening. I was unaware of meals and routines. Everything was gray. I didn't try to fight the truth, I just floated above it.

When Brian came he carried on as usual, telling me the news of the day. I stared past him, looking at the wall through his shadow.

"Hey, Sal, what's the matter?" he said finally. "You're so low tonight. Has something upset you?"

He had to repeat it twice, raising his voice a little impatiently, before I looked at him.

This was it. It was over.

"Brian," I spoke calmly as though talking about the weather, "Dr. Wood told me I would never walk again. He told me I would never be able to use my fingers." It was an effort to speak. I felt lifeless.

"Aw, Sal, you mustn't give up. You know they can't say for sure. No one knows. I thought we were going to prove all these doctors wrong." He looked into my eyes, but I was trying to shut him out. "Where's my old fighter, my tough guy?" he asked gently, pretending to punch my shoulder.

My eyes filled with tears and I began to choke on some phlegm caught in my throat. I wanted to tell him to go away and let me die. I'd never be anything but an invalid. But I couldn't speak.

"You're going to be okay, Sal. They do great things at these rehabilitation centers. Look at all the stories we've heard."

"Brian," I said with as much strength as I could. "Look at me! I won't let you waste your life. It'll be only a matter of time before you realize you don't love me. Why don't you just leave?"

Brian's face tightened up. He wiped my tears with the corner of his sleeve.

"Because I love you and I'm not going anywhere." He sat back and, holding my fingers, went through the routine finger exercises Sara had shown him weeks before. Neither of us spoke. Instead we stared at my hand in his.

I began quietly. "You know, I haven't been able to forget what Mrs. Holt said to me a few days after I came to Neuro."

"Who's Mrs. Holt?" he asked, bending my wrist.

"One of the nurses."

"What did she say?"

I felt the hate I'd felt since the first time I saw her. She had come into my room, closed the door and lit a cigarette. She leaned against the window ledge and flicked the ashes into an arrangement of mums.

"Quite an assortment of flowers you have here. You'd better enjoy them because they'll probably be your last."

I watched her with distaste, saying nothing.

"You'd better not count on your visitors coming around for too long, either. You know, lots of patients don't have any visitors, but then they've been sick for a while. Most folks don't like sick people. They get tired of visiting. You'd better learn to be by yourself." She glared at me. I tried to ignore her, wishing she would leave.

She continued, "Your boyfriend's a good-looking fellow. He may love you now, but wait until he finds out what a quad is. I've seen it so many times. When he realizes that your injury is forever he'll vanish. Surely you don't expect him to stick around?"

I watched, mesmerized as she butted her cigarette into the dirt. She walked over to the dresser and poked at a few of the stuffed animals friends had brought.

"If you had any sense you would tell him to go and

live a normal life. Save yourself, and him, a lot of pain."

I tried to scream at her. Get out! Mind your own damn business. But I was stunned by her words, knowing they were true.

Brian's face froze in anger. "Why didn't you tell me this before?"

"I knew it would make you angry and I didn't want to believe her."

"Well, don't. People who speak trash like that are nothing but trash themselves!"

His anger reached out to me, soothing my fears.

"I don't want to talk about this anymore." Brian picked up my arm and locked it in an arm-wrestle position. "Now, let's see your stuff."

It was his way of changing the mood without having to talk. He always let me win, but only after making me work, and it was obvious that I was getting stronger. I felt better and tried to push Dr. Wood's words out of my mind.

The next six weeks passed as dead time does. The ice tongs came out and a soft collar was placed around my neck. Gradually the head of my bed was raised until I was almost sitting up. I was introduced to the occupational therapist, who taught me how to use a hand splint to hold a fork, a toothbrush and a hairbrush.

I had often looked at children and thought what a shame it was that they couldn't remember the first few years of their lives. Now I knew why God had made it that way. Those early years of frustration and humiliation are too painful to remember.

However, he had given me a second chance and this time I would never forget.

"You've got to be patient," Rosey said during a visit. "Don't forget you've been lying down now for three months. It'll take time for your body to adjust."

"I am so sick of hearing that, Rosey," I snapped. "Everything takes time! I've been looking forward to getting out of this rotten bed for so long, and the minute I do I get all dizzy and scream to be put back to bed. And did you see the crazy getup they've got me wearing? I've got on old-lady stockings because my feet swell up, a girdle around my diaphragm to help me breathe, this stiff Elizabethan collar," I wave in the direction of an ugly mass of pink plastic, "and these charming hospital pants complete with Pampers. What if Brian had seen me? It would have been over for sure."

Rosey sat quietly for a moment.

"I love your wheelchair. They sure make them better these days. You wouldn't believe the old clunkers they used to have."

"I hated sitting in it. I felt as if my whole stomach was going to come out, and I couldn't focus on anything. I felt as if I was falling forward all the time and there was nothing to hold on to. It's like falling off a bridge or something."

"You'll see, every day will be a bit better." Rosey's voice sounded distant.

She had dark circles under her eyes, and her shoulders drooped.

How could she be so sad about losing her boyfriend? One she said she didn't even love. At least she could get up and walk around. She was pretty, smart, nice. She wouldn't have any trouble finding someone to love. I wished my problems were so small.

Suddenly I felt guilty.

"You're right, Rosey. And everything will be better for you. Have you heard from Robert?"

"No," she sighed. "I haven't even seen him. He must be going out of his way to avoid me."

"If he is, it's his loss."

Rosey smiled and reached out to pat my hand. "Thanks, Sally. When is Brian coming?"

"He should be here soon."

"Let me help you fix your hair. You do look a bit frazzled." She combed my hair forward in two pigtails so that the spots where the sides of my head had been shaved hardly showed. She pulled some lipstick and blush out of her purse and put them on me.

"There, you look great! It's wonderful to see you sitting up without those terrible tongs in your head." Rosey gave me a hug and then stood back to admire her work.

I knew I looked awful. My hair ends were dry and split, my face pale and thin.

"Yeah," I laughed, "as good as a sick anemic can. Oh, I can't wait to get outside into the fresh air, away from this stuffy building. I'm so tired of smelling disinfectant."

"When do you think you'll be going?"

"Soon, but," I mimicked in a sarcastic tone, "everything takes time."

For once time was on my side. The next day they told me I would be going to the Alfred Best Rehabilitation Center at the end of the following week. So many people had told me about the fantastic things they did for you at Best. I knew it was going to be hard work, that I was going to have a lot of therapy, but — I was going to learn how to be normal again.

I'd heard that Best was run more like a school than a hospital. You had to get around by yourself. No free rides.

Every day I sat in my chair for as long as I could. I spent hours pushing myself up and down the hall. At first every inch was painful. I would hook my right thumb into the rim of the wheel and swerve forward. Then I would do the same with the left. Swerve right, then left. Right then left.

As my balance became better I started to hook both thumbs at the same time. With a stronger push I would actually roll a bit on my own. Hook, push, roll. Hook, push, roll.

Finally I could keep the chair moving. It was still very slow and I had to stop every once in a while to rest my aching arms and thumbs, but I was moving in a semi-straight line.

Mother brought me some new slacks and sweaters and

helped me pack up all the things I'd collected over the past three and a half months. I was looking forward to getting up and dressed every day and was thankful for some new clothes. I knew Mom and Dad were as happy as I was and that we all expected the same miracles.

At last Friday arrived.

"Well, kiddo, we're going to miss you around here," Rosey said gently as she sat on the bed, facing me in my chair.

Suddenly I felt afraid. What was going to happen to me? This afternoon someone else would be in my bed and I would be somewhere new, where I would have to do everything for myself. How could I manage? More than three months had passed and I could hardly wheel the chair.

I'd felt all right until Sara came in to give me my last physio treatment. She brought me two books.

"I know you'll be okay," she said cheerfully. "I can't believe how much movement you've gained in your arms. And your wrist extensors are very strong. They'll improve your tenodesis, which enables you to form a grip, giving you more hand function. I think you may even regain the use of your triceps. I'm sure I can feel a flicker."

"My triceps!" I exclaimed.

"Yes, they'll really make a difference."

My God! I didn't want just my triceps. I thought this place was going to make me walk.

I had never forgiven Sara for her early diagnosis. Now

she was telling me I had made wonderful progress, that I might have the use of my triceps. I should feel happy? Instead I felt the old anger swell up inside me.

I thanked her for the books but hoped I'd never see her again.

Rosey slipped the two books into my case. While we were waiting for the transportation I told her what Sara had said.

"Sally, no one expects miracles from you. You must learn to do the most with what you have."

I stared at her in disbelief. Not Rosey, too.

"You don't think I'm going to get any better, either?"

"Of course you're going to get better," she said. "But you mustn't expect too much from yourself. You'll be surprised how strong and able you'll be."

I didn't like the sound of her words, but I wasn't going to dwell on them.

I'll show you all, I thought to myself.

"Dr. Wood didn't even come to say goodbye. I guess he thinks I'm just another sad case without any hope."

"Sally, don't be silly. You know how busy he is."

"Sure. It's not that I want to be special. I'd just like to feel like a person first and a patient second. Will everybody always think of me as a number, a name at the end of the bed? Someone you can't let yourself be friends with?"

"I'm your friend," Rosey said softly.

"And you've been wonderful," I said. "I don't know what I would have done without you."

At that moment the driver arrived to take me away from the neuro ward. The nurses all waved goodbye and Rosey came along to the elevator. She hugged me and promised to visit me on her first day off.

It was about an hour's drive from the hospital to the rehabilitation center. I had to bend down in the bus to see out the windows, but I didn't want to miss anything. It had been such a long time since I'd seen streets, buildings, parks and schools — places I remembered. The sun was shining and spring flowers decorated sidewalks and window boxes. The fragrance of blossoms blew in through the open window and I breathed deeply, ignoring the chill.

When we arrived at Best's I saw a group of women sitting by the front door. A large number of young people were sitting around smoking in the lobby, and a long lineup of people waited outside a closed door. Almost everyone was in a wheelchair.

I was going to school to learn how to be a gimp. A tightness pulled at my stomach and closed my throat.

I didn't want to go.

16

I LEARNED QUICKLY THAT gimpnology was a two-part course. The physical achievements came slowly with a lot of effort, frustration and not many signs of success. I knew I could never do the things they asked, so I felt defeated before I began.

That led to the second part, learning to accept the new me, this thing propped up by metal and rubber.

My reflection showed pale skin stretched over bone and framed with short neat hair. I had watched the long strands fall to the floor, not wanting to look in the mirror. I'd followed them as they were swept into the garbage, feeling that my whole past was being displaced. This person kept staring at me, but I shut her out. If I didn't look I wouldn't have to see, and I could still be me.

"Hi, you must be Sally. We've been expecting you. I'm Judy." Her friendliness broke over her face in a smile. Her hair, the color of wheat, cascaded halfway down her back. Her uniform was pale blue, a perfect match to her eyes.

I liked her instantly even though beside her I felt like a frump.

"Let me push you to your room," she said, coming around behind me. "Can you manage to hold your suitcase?"

"Sure," I said, trying to wrap my arms around the case balanced on my lap.

Judy pushed me to the end of the hall and into a large, bare white room. My eyes went directly to the beds. Above each one was a circular overhead bar attached by metal poles to the head of the bed.

"What are those?" I asked, horrified.

"The overhead bars? They're used to help you sit up."

"You mean I'm always going to have to have them?"

Judy took the case off my lap and rested it on the bed.

"That will depend on how good you are," she said kindly. "Lots of quads can get in and out of bed without them."

The word "quad" echoed painfully in my head.

"Well, I don't want them."

She flicked her long hair off her shoulders and looked at me seriously.

"Then you're going to have to work hard. Can I help you put your things away?"

"Yes, please," I said in a voice just above a whisper, my emotions building up in my throat.

"Your roommate, Sharon, is twenty-six. She's also a quad. She's at her classes now. You'll probably meet her before dinner. She's a nice girl, but very quiet. I think you'll like her."

I watched Judy as she unpacked the case, putting things where I could easily reach them. She was tall and strong-looking but she was graceful. I hoped we could become friends.

"Judy," I said timidly.

She turned around from the closet where she'd hung my new slacks. "Yes."

I looked from her face to my knees.

"Please don't call me a quad. It's such an ugly word."

She thought for a moment and sat down on the edge of the bed so that she was looking straight at me and not down at me.

"Sally, I'm afraid you're going to have to get used to it, especially around here. It's part of the vocabulary, an easy identification. But I understand how you feel and I will try. Now, you have a doctor's appointment in five minutes so you'd better get going."

"Where do I have to go? Don't they come here?"

"The doctors come on rounds once a week, but if you have something special you have to go to their offices. You'll have your admittance checkup. The offices are on the main floor to the right of the lobby. They're easy to find, but if you get lost just ask at the front desk." She reached into her pocket and pulled out a piece of paper. "You are to see Dr. Granger in room 198. I'll see you later."

With that she turned and left.

My God, I thought. It will take me five minutes to maneuver this chair down the hall, let alone downstairs. She could at least have taken me to the elevator.

I looked down at my hands. They were cracked and dry from the dirt on my wheels, and as I couldn't grip the wheel they kept slipping off. Hooking my thumb into the rim and pushing hard with one hand and then the other, I weaved down the hall like a drunk.

Before I had gone halfway I thought my arms were going to fall off. I finally arrived feeling broken and deflated.

I looked through the glass wicket, too exhausted to say my name.

Instead of praise for my accomplishment, the nurse scowled at me.

"The doctor is waiting."

The door opened and a tall, broad man in a brown tweed suit filled the doorway. He stepped aside, motioning me to come in. As my wheels hit the carpet my chair stopped dead.

I struggled to keep my head and shoulders from crumpling. I felt like jelly about to spread all over my chair and onto the floor.

"Here, let me help you," the doctor said, as he guided me into the room.

The examination was the same as all the others. He asked the same questions, pricked me with his pin, felt for lost muscles. He opened my blouse and listened to my heart. He took off my shoes and tested my reflexes.

When he had finished he pushed me into the hall with my shoes in my lap and my blouse undone.

"The nurse will fix you up." He rested his hand on my shoulder and with a smile of dismissal he went back into his office and closed the door.

Crumpled and slumped, I felt humiliated and beaten. A group of people passed me in the hall but paid no attention. I looked down through tears at my useless body.

Why should they help me? That's all I am, a mass of useless nothing. I imagined myself drowning, sinking to the bottom of a warm darkness.

"Sally," a slightly familiar voice echoed from a distance. "I wondered where you'd gotten to."

I recognized Judy's pretty face. She reached for my shoes and bent down to put them on my feet. She did up my blouse and straightened me up. "There, that's a bit better."

"Thanks," I muttered, hating myself and what I had become.

"How about a quick tour?" Judy said.

"Sure," I sighed, not caring what I did or where I went.

As Judy pushed me through the various departments I was glad she didn't try to introduce me to everyone. She leaned over, quietly telling me what was done in each area and who the people were. As I would either have had to turn around for her to hear me, which I couldn't do, or speak loudly, which I didn't want to do, I said nothing.

At the end of the tour she returned me to my room.

I felt so uncomfortable in this sterile room that would be my home for I didn't know how long. I listened to the muffled hum of a television down the hall. I could also hear a high-pitched wailing, almost like a siren. It seemed to be getting louder, coming closer to my room. It broke into a loud scream and then I realized it was someone calling.

"Nnnnuurrse," it was calling. Someone wanted the nurse. I turned to face the hall. I could hear footsteps running. The wailing was right outside my door.

I wheeled myself to the door and saw a woman crawling sideways on the floor. Her feet and arms were flying around as she used all her effort to call out. Her face was contorted, almost inhuman. There was something other than pain behind her eyes.

Judy and another nurse rushed to her. Judy steadied the woman while the other nurse hurried to fetch a wheelchair.

"Marta," Judy said gently, "where are you going?"

Marta tried to point and speak, but nothing came out except grunts.

An orderly came to help lift Marta back into her chair. She looked more human sitting up as the nurses tried to straighten her out and calm her down.

She had to be in her forties. She had a flat, round face and her black hair had been cut in the shape of a bowl, completely without style. She was thin and bony and had great difficulty controlling her arms and legs.

She held her head sideways, tilting it up to look at Judy. When she tried to speak, it seemed as if her mouth was full of marbles. Her tongue rolled uncontrollably, releasing only grunts and spit.

Judy wheeled her away into the room next to mine. I sat staring after them.

I was still sitting in the hall when Judy came out of Marta's room.

"Can I do anything for you, Sally?" she asked, as though nothing had happened.

"No," I answered, and then couldn't help myself. "What is wrong with her?"

"Don't worry about Marta. She won't bother you. Come into your room and I'll tell you about her."

Judy pushed me into my room and sat on my bed.

"Marta, I'm afraid, is a very sad case. She was hit by a car when she was about twenty-two and suffered a severe head injury. There is nothing we can do for her so she's waiting to be accepted into a home. She won't be here very much longer."

"How old is she?"

"Twenty-six."

"Twenty-six?"

"Yes, isn't it a shame? She was a model, a beautiful girl.

She has a picture of herself beside her bed. You should look at it sometime. She was hit crossing the street."

"What was she doing on the floor?"

"She was having a rest so Susan took her chair down to the brace shop to be repaired. She was upset because when she woke up she couldn't see it."

"Can she get herself into it?"

"No, she needs help. It just upset her that it wasn't there."

Judy stood up. Her smile was warm but I still felt rotten.

"Gee, Sally, I'm sorry this had to happen on your first day here. You haven't had a very nice welcome. This place is really not so bad. Please don't let Marta upset you."

But Marta did upset me. When Brian came I couldn't hold back the tears.

"Sal, it's not so bad. It's a hundred percent better than City. It's more like a school than a hospital."

"Not so bad," I screamed. "It's awful!"

Brian sat down on the single bed jutting out into the room and pulled my chair over beside him. He reached for my hands and began exercising my fingers.

"I know it seems awful, but it's just because it's new. Soon you'll be going to your classes all day and you won't have time to think about the bad things."

"What do you know?" I cried. "I'll tell you — nothing. I've got lots of time to think. All I have to do is think. You've only been here for a few hours, so it may seem peachy to you. But I have to stay here all day and all night. I've got lots of time to think about everything, and everything is bad."

"Honey, you haven't even been here a day. Give it a chance. You'll make friends with the other patients. At least you don't have to be in bed all day anymore."

"Terrific," I said sarcastically. "I don't want to make friends with the other patients. I want normal friends that do normal things. I don't want to be a gimp in a gimp's world."

Brian put my hand back firmly into my lap. His eyes turned cold.

"You're going to have to stop feeling sorry for yourself. What makes you think you're any better than the others in here? You're normal, and so are they."

"Normal! This place isn't normal, it's sick. Sick like my neighbor. She's dandy. She crawls along the floor screaming. I'll bet she screams half the night."

"Sally, nobody thinks it's going to be easy. But you can't let it get you down. You've got to be positive." His voice became less sharp. "Remember, we decided we're going to beat this thing, together."

"Together? We can't do it together."

"We sure as hell can try. Now, before I get angry, let's go for a tour. I want to see this 'awful' place."

A week later Brian and I sat silently in the dayroom staring at one another. He'd told me everything that had happened to him that day and any other gossip he could think of. As usual, he started off cheerfully but gradually my unresponsiveness got to him. I nodded or tried to smile, but mainly I just watched him. I was conscious of everybody else in the room and what they were saying.

Over in the corner a mother was trying to feed her son. He had a bib around his neck. He was at least seventeen, of a good height, and was making terrible faces at the cold food.

Why don't they let him die? He doesn't even know who he is.

At the table two quads were playing cards as well as they could.

Here we were, all one big happy family.

"Don't you have anything to say?" Brian interrupted my thoughts. "You're like talking to a blank wall."

"I don't feel like talking."

"Great. So I'm supposed to talk to myself?"

"I'm sorry. If only we could do something. Go somewhere, so we don't always have to talk. I wish we could sit in a comfortable chair and watch TV or something."

"We can go to the TV room if you like."

I could tell by his voice that he didn't want to do that any more than I did.

"You know darn well there'll be a bunch of people in there all lined up in rows. I meant somewhere by ourselves."

"Maybe you'd be happier if I wasn't here. It sounds as if I'm imposing on you."

"You know it's not you," I snapped. "It's just this place. I don't know why you all keep pretending it's so great. Do you think I've lost my mind? Well, you're the one who's lost your mind. I know you can't stand it here. No one could, so why do you keep coming around?"

"I come because I like to be with you. You used to be glad to see me. You used to be fun to be with." He caught himself and sighed. "Come on, Sal. Don't let it get to you, to us. Let's not fight. We can't let it drag us down." And about twenty minutes later he went home.

The next day I sat staring out the window of my room. I felt despair break over me as I noticed my mother's car pull into the parking lot. I didn't want to hear again how wonderful this place was. I didn't want to see her. The thought of hiding from her quickened my heartbeat.

I tried to turn my chair in a hurry, but there wasn't enough space between the bed and the built-in desk and it crashed into the side of the bed. The jolt threw me forward and I grabbed at my chair to keep from falling over into my lap.

Stopped before I had begun.

Oh, well, I wouldn't have made it to the elevators before she parked her car and came up to the third floor. Besides, where would I go?

Mother came bustling around the corner with a big smile on her face.

"Hi, dear. I was visiting Mary and since I was so close

I thought I would pop in and see how you were doing."

"I'm fine, Mom."

Mother sat on the end of the bed and caught her breath.

"Mary was telling me about her sister Joan. Apparently she was here about two years ago and swears by the place. She couldn't walk at all and after six months she was walking with canes. Isn't that marvelous?"

"Mother, Joan has arthritis."

"Yes, it's wonderful what they can do these days."

I didn't say anything so she started to rattle on about what Mary was doing. I let her go on for a few minutes, then interrupted her.

"I have to go to therapy."

"Sally, I'd like to come and watch."

"I'd rather you didn't."

"I'm interested in what you're doing. I won't bother you. I'll watch quietly."

"Yes, you *will* bother me." I paused and looked sadly at my mother. "It's hard enough without an audience."

Mother stood up and started to push my chair.

"Don't push me," I suddenly yelled. "I'm supposed to wheel myself."

She stepped back and raised her hand to stop me from saying anything more.

"All right, I'm going. I'll see you tonight."

"Look, Mom, I don't want you and Dad to come and see me every night."

"But, honey, we want to. Your father and I like coming to see you."

The silence between us was awkward.

There was no kind way to say this.

"Well, I don't like seeing you."

For a second a hurt look flashed across her face. She recovered quickly. "Now, dear, of course you do. I can't let you live in this place alone."

"I'm not alone. I'm surrounded by gimps and well-wishers."

"Sally, you mustn't speak like this. We're your family and we want to be near you."

I stared at my mother's set face. There was no reasoning with her.

The next day I phoned home.

"The volunteers are taking some of us to a movie so you don't need to bother coming tonight," I said to my mother, even though I had no intention of going to the movie.

I sat by the phone waiting for Brian to call, planning to tell him the same thing. I half expected him to say he'd like to come, too. I mean, we hadn't been out since the accident. This was a big step for me and I was sure he'd want to be there.

I was all ready to tell him that this was something I had to face alone.

I was almost talking myself into going. But I didn't really want to go anywhere, especially on the gimp bus.

What if someone saw me, someone who didn't know what had happened to me? God, I'd probably burst into tears. No. I wasn't going anywhere, and I didn't want to see anyone.

When Brian finally called he didn't ask to come. He almost sounded relieved.

Well, good. It was about time he got back to a normal life, and that wouldn't include me.

Rosey was the one person whose visits I still cherished. Then I learned she was going away.

"But, Rosey, you don't love him. Why do you have to go so far to be with someone you don't love?"

Rosey stared out across the city at the mountains. The sun was dropping into the ocean and brilliant shades of pink streaked the sky.

"New Zealand," I said. "You may never come back!"

I pulled at the Velcro that held my pusher mitts on my hands. The sound ripped through me. I couldn't hold back the tears.

"I need you, Rosey. What will I do without you? Please don't go."

She turned away from the sunset and dropped into a chair facing me. I was taken aback by the pain in her eyes.

"Sally, you'll be okay. You're surrounded by people who love you."

"But I need you."

"You need your parents. You need Brian. Sally, don't shut them out."

"They don't know me. They love somebody else." Large drops rolled down my cheeks. "They don't understand."

"They're trying to." She sounded far away. I felt as though she had already gone. "Sally, I have to get away. I can't take it anymore."

"Me?" I choked out. "You have to get away from me?"

"Aw, honey, not you, but the whole thing. I get too involved. I see it happening every day." I looked up from my hands and saw that she was crying, too. "I don't love Bob because I haven't let myself love him. I'm so entrenched in my work, I don't have anything left for romantic love. It seems so trivial compared with all the injured people reaching out to me. I've been pushing important people — people who love me, people who can show me some happiness — out of my life. Just as you're doing. You make me see that I'm wasting something very precious. There will always be people who need me, but there may not be another Bob. He loves me the way Brian loves you, and I've got to give him a chance." Reaching into her pocket she pulled out a tissue and stuffed it between my tight fingers.

Her touch was magnetic.

"You're my friend now and we'll always be friends, but you must help me. Every time I see a broken bone I feel it, too. I hurt all over. I've found myself crying in the washroom once too often."

I knew what she meant. In Intensive Care I'd felt the

pain of others, too. Still, I hated the sick people who were driving Rosey away. I hated Bob for taking her away. I hated God for letting all this happen. Most of all, I hated myself.

"If things don't work out I'll do some traveling and be home in six months. Otherwise Bob's internship will be over in two years." She reached over and squeezed my hand. "Please be happy for me."

"I am, Rosey," I lied. "I am."

* * *

My parents only came twice a week now. I had convinced them that I needed time to be by myself, and time to be alone with Brian. He always tried to be supportive, to encourage me to have faith. He tried to make me happy. If only he'd been honest with me. Rosey told me he had broken down at the hospital. If only he'd held me and we could have cried together. But, no, he had to be this tower of strength. Our relationship had become one big fake.

I still loved him. I knew that, but he wasn't right for me anymore. I wasn't good enough for him.

The last evening I saw Brian we were sitting at the table in the day room.

"Do you want to go down for some coffee?" Brian asked.

"No, it will keep me awake," I snapped.

"How about a game of cards?"

"I can't hold the cards."

"You could use a card holder."

"I don't want to."

"You're in a fine mood."

"Well, what do you expect?"

"I was hoping you'd be glad to see me."

"Well, I'm not."

"Come on, Sal, when are you going to let go?"

"Can't you see that's what I'm trying to do?"

I could see hurt on Brian's face. It pulled at the knot in my stomach.

"Look, Brian, can't you understand? It's no use. It won't work. I can't bear the thought of you spending the rest of your life with a gimp. You've got your whole life ahead of you. What if I can't have children? I'd always be wondering if you resented me, or worrying that you wished you could be with normal girls." I was speaking quickly. I paused to catch my breath. "I can't feel anything," I shouted at him.

Brian slammed his hand on the table.

"Damn you," he roared.

The fury startled me and frightened back my tears. Brian stood up and looked out the window. I felt numb all over.

Suddenly he turned back to me. His voice was low and he was trying to keep it steady.

"Sally, I'm not asking you to marry me. We're not ready to make that decision. We weren't ready before the

accident and we're not ready now, but I still love you."
He sat down and put his hand over my limp fingers. "I
want to share things with you. You haven't changed.
You're still the same person I care about."

"No, I'm not." I stared down at his hand, unable to
pull mine away. I began to sob as I looked up at him.
Each word was an effort, and my head jerked when I
spoke. "I'm not the same. I can't move and I can't feel.
How can you love me?"

Brian spoke softly. "Right now I wonder. If you want
my love like I want yours, we have to keep our sanity. We
have to fight together."

His smile infuriated me.

"Well, I don't want your love or your fight."

"How can you be so selfish? You're not the only one
who's hurting."

"Yes, I am. I'm the one who can't walk. It's my life
that's ruined, not yours. I can't bear the thought of people feeling sorry for you. 'Poor boy. Look what he's stuck
with.' Well, you're not stuck with me. Why don't you just
turn around and WALK away."

Brian stood up and turned to leave.

"When you stop feeling sorry for yourself, call me."

"Good," I yelled at his back. "Go on, get out of here.
It's about time you got smart."

Three

17

"SURE I FEEL SORRY for myself, and why shouldn't I?"

I slam the drawer on Brian's smiling face. But it lingers in my mind.

If you loved me so much, where have you been for the past three months? I gave you your chance to go and you took it. I'm not going to beg you to come back.

I lean forward on the desk and balance on my elbows.

Have you found someone else? Did you find a job closer to town this year, or are you away in the woods somewhere?

I close my eyes. It's easy to picture Brian working in the forest. I can see him in his red lumberman's shirt, bending over, planting a tiny seedling. His boots are muddy and he's grimy.

I used to sit at home on Friday nights waiting to smell the scent of evergreen and earth that still clung to him.

Now someone else is waiting for him.

I'm so mixed up I don't know how I feel. Am I jealous? Angry? Do I want him to come back? If I don't, why am I so unhappy? Like my veins, punctured and weak from all the blood tests, my heart is deflated and withered.

Looking out the window, I notice Michael heading toward the parking lot. There are only two cars left. One is a flashy red one, a new model, and the other is an older type, like the old family car that you buy from an ad in the paper.

Michael goes toward the second one. It looks like him, dependable and practical. He faces me as he gets in.

I wish I could go with you. I wish you could take me away from here.

Later I poke at my food in the cafeteria. The meatloaf looks gray beside pale boiled potatoes. The others at the table have already finished, and the smoke from their cigarettes drifts across my food. My fork, caught in the dry meat, falls to my plate.

I was so proud of myself when I managed to eat without a hand splint. As long as the fork isn't too heavy or thick I can pry it between my fingers and manage to hold on. But every once in a while I lose my grip and drop it.

The fork lies on my plate covered in food. I push my plate away in disgust.

Jake calls for some coffee for me. It's a habit he still keeps up and it always makes me feel cared for.

I smile up at him.

"Don't worry, babe," he says. "How about if I take you to the White Spot?"

"Only a drive-in? Why not Trader Vic's?"

Jake reaches down and pulls a new card from his wallet. He flicks it across the table.

"You're looking at a man with wheels."

I know what this means to Jake — his ticket to freedom.

"Jake, that's fantastic! How did the test go?"

Jake had his car converted to hand controls about a month ago and has been taking special driver training through the center. It's the one class, besides his weight lifting, that he never misses.

He shrugs, and I see large muscles bulging beneath his faded black T-shirt.

"It was a snap. I could drive circles around the fool they sent out with me."

The shadow of his beard makes him look tough. I see pride in his deep blue eyes.

"I'll bet you scared him half to death," I laugh.

Jake draws deeply on his cigarette and laughs, too.

"Yeah, I took him for a ride. But it was the best ride he's been on. I wasn't about to give him a chance to fail me."

"You're rotten to the core," I say, smiling. "But I'm proud of you."

"How about it? Would you like to take a spin?"

"Come on, Jake. How would I get into the car?"

"You could use a sliding board. I'll pull you in from the other side."

I can feel frustration creeping up inside me. "And what about the chair?"

"We'll leave it here. What do we need to take the chair for?"

I realize he's serious. He really doesn't have any idea how hard it is to move me.

I suddenly feel jealous of his new freedom. It would be wonderful to get away from this place, but I don't want to be dragged around like a sack of dead weight. I'd have to get a nurse to help me get in and out. I don't need them watching over me any more than they already do. If I can't go by myself, I don't want to go.

"I've never done a car transfer. I don't know how."

I have been out with Dad. He was so nervous the first time — so afraid of hurting me. He lifted me up and put me in the car and it felt the way it did when I was little.

But Jake can't pick me up, and besides, I hardly want to feel like a little girl with him.

"Please don't be angry, Jake. I'm just not ready."

"Well, get ready. You're not trying hard enough, Sally. You're going to get left behind. If you want to stay in this hellhole, don't expect me to stick around with you." He snatches up his license and shoves it back into his wallet.

I swallow hard and look down at my cold food.

"I thought you understood," I whisper. "I thought you cared."

Jake puts his hands on the edge of the table, his fingers digging into the surface, and pushes his chair back.

"I do," he says. "Too damn much." He wheels quickly from the room.

* * *

I don't know how, but Michael and I have become
friends. I've stopped fighting him. He still pushes me and
I crab back, but it's different. Sometimes when I look at
him I can feel my heart turn over. My blood rushes
through me and I'm on fire.

I know we can never be more than therapist and
patient. He's too good at his job. He would never get
involved. Oh, he's nice to me and treats me like a friend
when I'm with him. He calls me Sal, squeezes my shoulder and makes me feel special. But I see him do that with
the others. He tries to make everyone feel special. It
makes me like him even more.

"Okay, wake up, it's time to roll. Quit stalling. Swing
your arms hard and use your head." Michael opens his
eyes wide as he repeats the same old lines.

"Do I have to?"

"Yes, on three."

"Come on, Michael, give me a break."

"I'll give you a break when you learn to roll."

I begin to rock my upper body, trying to gain momentum.

"I'll never be able to do it."

"Yes, you will. One, two, threeeee. Good try. Do it
again."

I've been trying to roll for a good four months now, and I don't seem to be any closer than when I started. However, I didn't think I would be able to get in and out of my chair and I mastered that. I know that rolling will be a good skill for me, especially for dressing and moving in bed.

The image makes me think of Brian, and I remember the night at Star. I remember feeling him lying beside me in our semi-nakedness. Our bodies loose and free, lying so close, touching, melting together. We were so aware of every inch of our bodies, mine and his.

I watch Michael as he puts on my shoes at the end of the session. His broad shoulders and muscular arms are solid, and his shirt is stretched tightly over them.

I wonder what it would be like to have his arms wrapped around me, like being wrapped inside a mountain.

"Michael, will you answer me something honestly?"

His smile is infectious. "Yes, if I can."

"Do you think I could manage to get into a car myself?"

Sitting on the mat he thinks for a minute.

"Yes, if you had the right car with fairly wide doors and a seat level to your chair. The old kind are usually the best."

"Could you show me what to do?"

"I think so. Actually, my car would be good. It's one of those old fossils."

"I know, but I like it. It suits you."

Michael throws out a laugh. "An old fossil, am I?" He tries to look offended. "Have you been spying on me?"

"No. I just hate it when you leave."

Why did I say that, I scream at myself.

Michael sits watching me for a minute, making me feel awkward. I know he's surprised. The thought of me liking him is probably a joke to him. There's no way he'd ever like me.

"How about a Camaro?" I ask, thinking of Jake's car.

"I'm not too sure. You'll have to try before you know. You're not wanting to go gallivanting around with Jake Thomas, are you?"

"What's it to you?"

"I didn't think he was your type."

It isn't like Michael to judge people. I don't want to talk to him about Jake.

"I'll take anybody who will have me. Look, will you help me or not?"

"Of course I'll help you. Starting next week I've got a spare block on Monday, Wednesday and Friday at four. I'll schedule you for a transfer class. Actually, I've got a few other people who could join us."

I feel glad and disappointed at the same time. Glad that I'll have some extra time with Michael, and sad that there will be others.

What are these feelings I have for Michael? Did I really think he might want to spend some extra time alone with me? What does he think about me now?

I know it's only a game I'm playing, but the game feels good and gives me something to look forward to. My feelings for Jake are real, but I'm confused about them, too. Two gimps trying to make it together? What a joke!

On Monday at four o'clock I wait in the lobby for Michael to bring the car around. A flat piece of thin wood about three feet by one foot lies balanced on my lap. I sanded the edges to make it free of splinters.

It wasn't because I wanted to. My occupational therapist is always looking for projects to improve my hand skills. I've done it all, from découpage to pottery. Every time I need an aid I'm encouraged to assemble it myself or at least sand it and paint it. I asked for a sliding board and before I knew it I was sanding.

Getting into the car isn't really that difficult. Michael shows the others, two paras, and they have no trouble at all.

When it's my turn I manage to park my chair alongside the passenger seat, and that's as far as I can go. I can't lift my leg high enough to throw it into the car. Then I can't get a grip on the sliding board to slip it under my bottom to make a flat path.

Michael shoves the board under me. Once it's in the perfect position I twist around to face the door and, pushing on the door, I slide into the car.

Inside the car I can't reach my second leg, which is still dangling outside. Michael pulls the board out from under me and gives me a big grin.

"Nothing to it."

"Am I supposed to be able to pick up the chair now and throw it in the back seat?"

I know this much because I've watched Jake do it himself.

"That's what most people do, but I think you should concentrate on getting yourself in first."

"In other words, you don't think I can do it?"

"The chair is pretty heavy, Sally. But if you work hard enough you may be able to do it. If not, you can always ask someone to throw it in the trunk for you."

"And when I get to the other end?"

"I guess you'll have to hail someone else." He gives me a little wink. "With that pretty face you shouldn't have any trouble."

I stare at the dashboard with a pout on my face.

"Now, to get out, leave your feet in the car. Turn and push with one hand on the dashboard and one hand on the car seat. Once you're back in your chair you can lift your legs out of the car."

Michael slides the board under my bottom again and I push myself out of the car. We go through the movements, in and out, two more times. The only part I can do is the pushing and the sliding. I know the rest is impossible.

Slumped over in the car, I feel exhausted. I let my head and shoulders droop. The sun streams in through the windshield and the warm air is comforting and relaxing.

"How about a ride?" I'm stalling to rest my aching arms.

Michael looks at me and then at his watch.

"I have to pick up Barbara at the university. You could come. Wait here and I'll tell the desk what we're up to." He leans across me and buckles the seatbelt.

Sitting in the car like a real person, I suddenly feel wonderful. There is no chair, only me.

We drive along the shore in the direction of the university. The windows are down and warm air blows my hair away from my face.

I have to catch my breath at the beauty around me. Scattered sailboards are drifting peacefully in the bay. A few large freighters are moored, looking strong and massive. In the background the mountains separate the pale sky from the deep rippling sea.

How can all this still be here? Has it been here the whole time?

A little boy is pulling a wagon filled with the evening papers. His dog is running happily beside him. Michael has to swerve a little to give them room. I want to wave at the boy, to get out and pull his wagon.

This is the real world, the world I knew. I want to be a part of it. I am living in a nightmare waiting for the day when I can come back to this. It's right here. It's been here all the time.

How can God let it happen? It's not fair that one person can be sailing, laughing as he feels the warm salty air against his skin, while someone else is locked in a white-walled world of pain and horror. But should the world stop because I can't walk? That wouldn't make me feel better. I still wouldn't ever walk again. I've been waiting for God to make me better, but why should he cure me and not the others?

I feel a heaviness come over me. I know I'm not going to be walking anywhere. But even though I may never be that man in the sailboat, I sure as hell can sit on the beach.

"Michael, could we sit by the beach for a few minutes?"

There's a single row of parking spaces between the road and the beach. Michael pulls in and turns off the motor. He relaxes into the corner and lays his arm along the back of the seat. I'm aware of his hand almost resting on my shoulder, but I don't look at him.

I feel a dry ache in my throat. My heart drones in my ears. The tide is out, and flat sand reaches far out to the water. I remember how hard it was to run in the sand, feeling it shift beneath me, pulling on my thighs.

Michael interrupts my thoughts.

"Sally, are you all right? Are you comfortable?"

I realize I've been quiet.

"I'm fine," I answer. "How can you work there, Mike? Doesn't it ever get to you?"

"I like it. I like the people I work with."

"The staff, or the patients?"

"Both."

"But the patients are usually so horrible, like me." I keep my eyes on the sailboats.

"Sally," he moves his hand onto my shoulder and gives it a friendly squeeze, "you haven't been horrible."

"I haven't exactly been a ray of sunshine."

"No. I know it's not easy for any of you. I don't expect you to be happy about what's happened. It's my job to help you get back as much as you can. If I can make your life a little easier, then that makes me happy."

"But there's always more. It keeps happening. Doesn't that bother you?"

"People recover, Sal. They learn what they can do and then they get on with life. Most people go out a better person than they came in. I wouldn't wish it on anybody, but it brings out strength in people."

"It brings out some pretty bad things, too."

"It's a way of fighting. They usually get over it."

We sit quietly for a moment. Am I getting over it? I think back over the past few months. I've been so angry and full of hate.

A new determination stirs within me. I am tougher than that. How could I let myself be so weak and not able to see it?

"Mike, do you ever make friends with your patients?"

Michael flashes me a grin. "I like them to consider me a friend. I don't really think of them as patients. After all, they're not sick." He pauses. "Of course, I feel closer to some than others."

"Do you ever see them once they leave the center?"

"Not usually." He notices my disappointment. "I become very attached to some of my patients, especially the ones who are at the center for a long time. But we're thrown together in an unreal world. I share their disappointments and watch them grow. I can't help them if I let myself get too close."

The air in the car is still warm. The smell of French fries drifts in from a nearby stand. I try to shift my weight but I'm anchored to the upholstery.

I can't go back to my old world. I don't fit in anymore. I feel frustration growing. It's pulling me down.

"Sally, you are a terrific girl." Michael's words are genuine but they twist in my stomach. "I like you and want to see you happy. But you have to be happy with yourself first. I will always be here when you need me."

"Oh, Michael." I turn toward the ocean, hoping he won't see my tears. They roll into my mouth, salty like the sea. "I'm so afraid."

He gives me a long squeeze. "It's going to be tough, Sal, but you've come a long way. It will be easier from now on."

In my mind I cling to his body. For the first time in ages I look into the future with hope.

At least I've run in the sand. I'll always have the memory.

Michael starts the car and we drive silently to the university.

18

"SALLY? SALLY?" AT FIRST I think I'm dreaming. "It's about Jake. I thought you'd like to know."

I hardly ever see Judy anymore. She's been going to summer school, completing her nursing degree, and has been working only nights. I'm always in bed when she comes on shift and usually asleep by the time she finishes listening to the daily report. She's so quiet and gentle that when she comes in to turn me I barely wake up. Her hands are warm, and she's careful not to let cold night air in under the covers.

We rarely talk, unless I can't sleep and she has a few minutes. Then she pulls a chair close to the bed and tells me about her course or where she went for the weekend. She knows about my days, she hears them on report, and she whispers to me that she understands.

It made me furious two months ago when she told me that she knew about Jake and me because it had been reported. I knew "they" didn't think he was good for me, but it bugged me that they sat around discussing it on a tape.

"Jesus, Judy, it's none of their damn business. Who do they think they are telling me who my friends should be?"

"They don't want you to make any foolish mistakes. You know Jake doesn't go to programs, and he's going to get kicked out for smoking dope. He's not exactly a good influence," Judy said.

"Did they send you in to talk to me?"

A red glow from the flashlight emphasized the worried expression on Judy's tired face.

"They're concerned about you, Sally. We all are. They know I'm your friend."

"Are you going to tell me to stay away from him, too?"

"I'm not going to tell you anything. I know you're okay. I only said I would talk to you."

"And what I say, will that go on report?"

Judy leaned forward. "Of course not."

No one has mentioned anything to me about avoiding Jake since. Now Judy is saying Jake's name.

"Sally, I must tell you about Jake."

I try to raise myself, then sink back into the pillow. I strain to see Judy's eyes.

"What's happened? Is he all right?"

She puts her hand on my shoulder.

"Tell me," I shriek.

"I think he's okay. He went out without a pass tonight. He came back after two a.m. stoned. Phil had been told not to let him in. He turned him away."

"Where do they expect him to go?" I feel angry.

"I don't know," she sighs. "He's strong, Sally. He'll manage."

"They're supposed to help him. How are they helping him by sending him off into the night with nowhere to go?"

"He doesn't help himself. This isn't a fraternity house. It's a hospital with patients, doctors and other professionals trying to work together. He won't work with us. Do you think getting high and driving around in that fast car is good for him?"

"Yes, it's a release, a step toward freedom."

"He may find himself free before he's ready. If I were you, I'd try and talk some sense into him."

"That's the last thing he wants to hear from me." I see Judy shrug. "But I'll try."

"Good." She pats me. I know she's concerned. "I'm sorry to trouble you at this hour but I wanted to tell you."

"Thanks. I'm glad you did."

God, Jake, where are you? Please be all right. Why didn't I go with you tonight? If you come back safely I promise I'll try.

I picture him sitting in an all-night bar. His chair is parked sideways so that he can be near the table. A half-drunk rum and Coke and an ashtray full of cigarette butts sit in front of him. His eyes, red from the smoke and the late hour, stare at the wall.

My mind wanders. Maybe he's driving around end-lessly. He used to tell me how whenever he felt anxious he would drive somewhere he'd never been before.

What will he do when he gets there? He has no money, no clothes, no medical supplies.

I wake up with morning sun making the whole room shine. I can't remember falling asleep.

Jake. I must be near when he gets back. I must help him not be angry. He can't leave yet. He's not ready. I'm not ready to be left without him.

How can I get out of program? After self-care I'll just have to hide. Michael will come looking for me for sure. I can't wait in the lobby. He'll see me, and the loop and the courtyard are the first places he'll look.

I know, I'll hide around the corner near the parking lot and read in the sun while I wait.

I hurry through my established self-care routine. The O.T., Chris, only looks in on me from time to time to make sure I'm doing all right. She's sewn loops onto my bra so that by slipping my fingers into them I can hook up in front of me and then twist it around to my back. I always wear sweaters because they're easy to pull over my head.

After I've dressed my top half I slide onto the bed. Getting my legs into my slacks is the hardest part. Once my feet are through I wiggle my slacks up as far as I can while I'm in a sitting position. Then, while I carefully hold my balance, I slip my wrists into loops on either side of my slacks. When I have a good grip I let myself fall back onto the pillow, pulling hard on the loops. As I fall back my hips rise and I yank my pants up to my waist.

The harder I throw myself back the more momentum I get and the easier my pants slide up. But I must wear slippery underwear and slacks or nothing will slide. A ring on my zipper helps me to fasten up.

I push myself into my chair and call for someone to help me put on my socks and shoes, the only part I have left to conquer.

It usually takes me about thirty minutes, but this morning I'm finished in twenty. I quickly brush my hair and stab at my mouth with my lipstick.

As I wheel through the front doors I feel a wave of relief as fresh morning air rolls over me. I hope no one has seen me.

It's a little harder wheeling on the pavement, but I hurry to get myself out of sight. My heart is beating hard and I feel a little silly. Brian would tease me. He'd call me Super Snoop, because I always loved an adventure, especially one that called for sneaky measures.

Turning my chair I roll backwards until my wheels hit the wall. I push on my brakes and sigh.

Peering through the leaves of a flowering bush, I look back at my path.

There is no one around and I doubt anyone can see me. The delicate blue flowers clustered together in a pom-pom give off a gentle fragrance. They remind me of a giant dandelion puff, and I wonder whether blowing would scatter the petals.

I close my eyes, breathe deeply to catch my breath and lift my face up to the warmth of the sun. It's like a soothing blanket, and I hold still, absorbing its magic.

Now, if only Jake comes back soon. I feel as if he's been gone for days.

I hear a shuffle on the pavement. My head jerks down as I peer through the bush.

It's another patient, an older man who's had a stroke. He's using his good foot to drag his chair along while he guides it with his right hand on the rim. The other hand lies in his lap, tucked against his body to hide its uselessness. His left foot is just there, resting on the pedal. On his face is a look of agony as he heads in my direction.

Go away, I say to myself.

As he drags himself past the bush, his shoulders are leaning forward, and he's stooped by his effort. His eyes look up at me from his hunched body.

At first he's startled to see me. Then half of his mouth lifts in a smile. He gropes to say something. His words are muffled, his tongue dead.

Go away. Leave me alone, I can't talk to you. You're pathetic.

He opens his mouth and blows out a low grunt. My God, he's trying to say hi.

"Hi," I breathe the word for him as well as for myself.

"Haaah." He drags his arm across his mouth to wipe a bit of drool.

I want to pull his chair back out of sight.

"Here. Pull your chair around this way, against the wall. It's nice in the sun." I have no choice.

His maneuvers are slow, worse than mine, but his one leg is strong and he manages.

"There. Now, can you sit up straight? Put your head back, close your eyes, feel the sun." It's hard for him to hold his head back, but I see a flicker of pleasure and a release of tension. I'm aware of a sense of power. "Isn't it a lovely day?"

He nods his head, which is beginning to droop.

"Naah." He shows his one-sided smile, but his eyes are heavy with sadness.

Actually he's not that old, maybe in his late fifties. A little older than my father. In my mind I try to stand him up, make him strong and whole. I tell him my name, where I live and about my family. I ask him questions about himself and try to make words from his replies. I don't understand, but I get better as I become used to him.

It grows too hot for him, and perspiration rolls down the side of his face. I can see he's tired.

"Maybe you should go in now. We can talk again another time."

I watch him as he slowly shuffles back around the ice-blue flowers.

How horrible it must be not to be able to speak. My initial reaction nags at me. How can I be so shallow, so selfish? I didn't stop to think that he was a person first.

How can I expect others to treat me like a normal person if I reject others who aren't perfect?

Jake, where are you? Please come back.

I look at my watch and see that it's only noon. I must get Mother to put my old strap back on. The thin gold bracelet has been replaced by a cheap expansion type so I can put on my watch myself. I don't know why my mother bothered because I have to get someone to wind it for me anyway.

I was so thrilled when Brian gave it to me for Christmas that I cried. Looking at it now I feel like crying again.

God, I feel awful. I'm not perspiring, but I'm dizzy and short of breath, as if I'm suffocating from the heat. I guess I've been in the sun too long.

I'd better go in. I'm not going to be able to stop Jake from doing anything or saying anything anyway. I know he wants to go. He's fed up.

I slowly turn and wheel into the building.

In the cafeteria I sip at my soup, being careful not to drop my spoon. I have two napkins spread across my lap. I hate being sloppy.

I'm facing the door, and I look up at each new person who comes in. Sharon is sitting across from me. I can feel her watching me.

"I guess you've heard about Jake?"

I almost drop my spoon.

"What?"

"He just got the boot."

"What are you talking about? He's not even in the center."

"He sure is. He just had a powwow with Granger. He's upstairs packing."

Granger! Oh, no. Once he sentences you there's no changing his mind. When did Jake get back? How did I miss him?

"Sharon, were you around when Jake got back?" I ask, undoing my brakes.

"No, but I was just up there. He's not very happy. Sal, why don't you finish your soup and give him a while to cool off?"

"It looks as though they haven't given him any time."

I can't get upstairs fast enough. I find Jake pulling his clothes out of a drawer, rolling them up in a ball and throwing them across the room to the bed. Some hit the lid of an old battered leather case and fall into it, some lie scattered on the bed, and a few have fallen to the floor.

"Jake, you can't go until you find somewhere to live."

"I'll find somewhere."

"Where will you go tonight?"

"The first place I'm going is somewhere I can have a drink in peace."

"Please don't go when you're so angry. Tomorrow things will be better."

"You're right, they will, but not around here."

"What did Dr. Granger say? Did he actually kick you out?"

"No, he didn't kick me out." Jake's voice is sarcastic. "He merely read me the rules. He said I'd just have to break one more and I could pack my bags. Well, I won't give him the satisfaction of throwing out."

I'm suddenly angry.

"Can't you see that people around here are trying to help you? This isn't a detention home. They're not trying to punish you. It's a place to get better."

Jake's jaw is rigid, and every muscle in his face is tight.

"Since when did you change sides? I thought we were in this together."

"We are, Jake. In the past couple of weeks I've begun to see that we've been blinded by our own hate. We've been too involved with our own feelings to understand what's happening around us. Sure this place is a drag. I hate it as much as you do. I hate every rule and every damn nurse or orderly who throws it in my face." I lean forward, gripping my armrests. "But they're trying to help us. We've got to let them. We don't have a choice."

"I have a choice and I'm leaving. There's an empty room at the Para Lodge. I'll stay there until I can find an apartment. Then I'll get a job."

"What kind of job?"

"Don't worry, I'll find one." He stuffs everything into the case and slams the lid shut. "Look, Sal, it'll be great. You can come over and we can smoke up every night.

There'll be no one to bug us. It's time for me to move on. I'm not getting any stronger, I'm only wasting time."

I know this is the end of us. I don't want to smoke with Jake anymore. Dope makes me feel lazy and I want to get going, to get on with living.

I watch the blue eyes that I've loved over the past months.

"Oh, Jake, I'll miss you so much."

"Aw, Sal, don't cry. I have to go."

"I know," I whisper.

He wheels over and kisses me. His day-old beard is rough against my skin and his breath is stale.

"I'll miss you, too, babe."

19

I DON'T WANT TO tell Dr. Ericson about Jake. My loneliness is all I have left of him and I don't want to share it, not yet.

"I have to get out of here," I tell him.

"Where will you go?"

"Home."

"Can you manage at home?"

"I won't need to."

"What will happen when you're at home?"

Ericson looks at me from across the desk. It's made of heavy oak, solid like him. I wonder if he ever gets up from his chair. I'm glad that he doesn't when I'm here, because it would make me feel small.

He's holding his pen above a blank piece of paper in front of him.

I say what he wants me to say.

"My mother will look after me."

"Is that what you want?"

"Yes." I wait for him to write. *Sally is lazy. She doesn't want to do things for herself. She wants others to wait on her.*

But he doesn't write. He waits for me to go on.

I wish there was a window in his office. There's nowhere for me to look, no escape from his eyes.

"She will eventually anyway. Listen, I'll never be able to do anything for myself, so I may as well start getting used to it now. Why should I struggle to do things that other people can do for me in a fraction of the time? My mother wants to do things for me, so why should I stop her?"

"Once you start letting people do things for you it will be harder for you to break away. It's all right to live with your parents, but you must set yourself up to be as independent as you can. Otherwise you'll never have a life of your own."

I haven't looked at the future. I've only let myself see my old future, the way I would have been.

I picture myself when I'm old, my mother even older with gray hair and stooping shoulders. She shuffles her feet as she brings me tea on a tray.

No, I don't want my mother to look after me forever.

"I've had it here. I can't do anything more today than I could yesterday."

"No, but you can do more this month than you could last month."

"Not much. I can get on and off a bed. I can put on most of my clothes. There isn't anything else for me."

Ericson tilts his head and shrugs slightly. Neither one of us speaks. I know I don't mean what I'm saying, and Ericson knows it, too. I feel as if I'm stuck in a blender and I can't shut it off.

"I can't help it. I haven't any choice."

"Sally, you are a young person. You have your whole life in front of you. You have a great many choices. You can continue with your schooling and find a suitable career. You can do something useful with your life. I know all these sound impossible, but they aren't. You have a lot to share with people and you mustn't shut yourself off. Have you ever thought about marriage?"

"Marriage belongs in the future of my past."

"Why?"

Now it's my turn to raise my eyebrows.

"Come on," I say. "No one wants to marry a gimp." My words sound as absurd as he wants them to.

Ericson returns the gesture and laughs. It's a nice laugh, deep and throaty, not telling me that I'm feeling sorry for myself, or that I'm stupid, but that everything is all right.

I laugh, too. We laugh together and it feels comfortable. I don't want to say anything or the moment will fade.

Ericson asks pleasantly, "Why do you think that no one could love you?"

"There are too many other girls to choose from. Why marry someone like me when you can lead a normal life with a normal wife?"

"Sometimes you can't help who you fall in love with."

"So, I should hang around hoping someone slips up?"

Ericson laughs again. "Well, as long as you know there's a chance."

"Even if I did love someone and I thought he loved me

back," I say, thinking of Brian, "I don't think it would be fair to marry him. There's a part of love that I can't fulfill."

"Sally, you can still have a very fulfilling, intimate relationship. That's the wonder of love. You would find a way to work it out. Sex certainly isn't, or shouldn't be, the foundation of any marriage."

I've heard these words before, from Mother, from Brian, from Jake. Somehow they seem more real coming from Dr. Ericson. I trust him. I know he's not just trying to make me feel better. He knows I need the truth.

But I can't believe someone could love me, not like this.

"What about children?" I ask. "Children are a part of marriage. How am I supposed to have children?"

"Sally, children may be possible. Now, you would have to have a checkup with a gynecologist, but I have known quadriplegics to have perfectly normal pregnancies and raise a family." He waits, giving me time to absorb his words.

I used to think that the worst thing that could happen to a woman would be to find out she couldn't have children. Not necessarily that she didn't have any, but that she didn't have the choice. I had postponed the worry, left it dangling beyond my reach. Dr. Ericson has cut the string, and it has fallen over me.

"You mean I could actually have a baby?"

Dr. Ericson smiles, and I can't blame him. Even to my own ears my voice sounds so incredulous that it's funny. He answers me seriously, though.

"I know it's possible. I think you should get the head

nurse to make an appointment for you. Then you can find out all about it, ask any questions that may be bothering you."

"I'd love a little girl. But how would I look after her? How could I hold her, pick her up? I can't even pick up a pencil."

The idea of a baby is like a miracle. I can see myself bending over a crib, reaching down and picking up a bundle of softness. I hold her to me. I cuddle her close, breathing in the scent of baby.

Suddenly I actually feel whole. I feel my blood rushing through me, my heart beating.

I can still be a woman.

"Do you really think so, Dr. Ericson?" I try to keep my voice calm.

Again a smile spreads across his face. I hold my breath.

"Sally, I know it's possible, but I think you should talk to the experts."

* * *

It's Wednesday, and I'm sitting in my room waiting for the doctors to come on their rounds. Since I'm at the end of the wing that they usually visit last, I have to sit and wait an hour, sometimes longer.

I hate the wait. It's such a waste of time.

I decide to fill the time by writing to Rosey. I don't write very much because I'm embarrassed about it. My letters are large and wiggly and every once in a while my pen slips, even though it's in a splint attached to my hand, and the letters shoot off in weird directions. It looks like the work of a third-grade student — a poor one at that.

I know Rosey doesn't really want to hear from me. I'm part of a world she's trying to forget. I'll always be the patient and she the nurse and that's a hard relationship to build a friendship on.

But I don't care. I miss her and I want to talk to her.

September 8, 1973

Dear Rosey,

I am sitting in my room waiting for the doctors to come on rounds. The air-conditioning is blowing in my face as usual, and I am freezing as I look out on a beautiful sunny day. I will never understand how they can allow a place like this to be so drafty when there are so many people here who are bothered by drafts.

I would love to be outside but, oh no, I have to wait for their lordships to come by and ask me about my bladder. I don't know why they can't just look on my chart, or better yet, listen to report. God knows they never listen to anything I say, so I don't know why they have to see me.

I hope you don't mind me writing to you. I often think about you and try to imagine what it's like in New Zealand. Is it as beautiful as all the pictures? I guess the weather is sunny and warm and that you are gorgeous and brown. I actually have a small tan. Small in that it is only on my hands, arms and face. My days of shorts and bathing suits are over. The trouble here is that if you wear something skimpy to sit in the sun, when you come inside you freeze to death. I have a nice line around my bulging biceps from my T-shirt. Quite attractive!

How is Bob? Is he enjoying his internship? I wonder whether he has managed to keep you out of the hospital. I'll bet not, knowing you're not comfortable unless you're dressed in white.

Do they have any type of rehabilitation centers around there? How about spinal cord units? I've heard they have a good one in Sydney. I guess you ship all your gimps there.

I haven't seen Brian for months. I know my mother is keeping tabs on what he's doing, but she never mentions his name. He could be in Timbuktu for all I know. He's probably fallen madly in love with some gorgeous girl and is glad to be rid of me.

Sometimes I think you were right, I should have tried harder to keep him around. I really am very lonely and can hardly bear to let myself think of him. But I had to give him a chance. If he loved me I would have heard from him. If he is the only real love I ever have, at least I have good memories.

I had a thing going with one of the patients here. His name is Jake and he's a para. He is a real sweet guy and really helped me to like myself a little better. However, he is a little wild for me and I worry about what will happen to him. He has left the center now and is staying at the Para Lodge. I've been to visit him a few times but I'm not too crazy about his friends. Also, he is heavily into dope and I don't belong in that scene. I tried it for a while, and I have to admit it sure made life more bearable, but it didn't seem to solve my problems and I hate to think of what it might be doing to my head. That's all I need, a little brain damage!

I have been working a little harder in physio lately and you won't believe this but I can almost roll. I can sit up in bed using the overhead sling, and getting in and out of my chair is a snap.

Michael, my physio, has been super. At first I couldn't tolerate him, he was so much like Brian, but now I see that that's not so bad. I know he has a serious girlfriend but I find myself watching him and accidentally on purpose bumping into him. He took me for a drive to the beach one afternoon and he made me feel wonderful. If only I thought there was a chance!

Dr. Ericson says he thinks there's a possibility I may be able to have kids. Not that I will ever get married, let alone have a baby, but knowing there is a chance makes me feel like a new person. I am going to see a gynecologist on Friday. I am so nervous I feel like wetting my pants. Bad joke!

I think I hear the gallery coming. Can you believe it, it's quarter past twelve and they're just coming now. There will be absolutely nothing left in the cafeteria but half-dead sandwiches.

If you have a minute I'd love to hear from you. I miss you, but hope you are well and happy.

Take care,
Sally

P.S. Sorry about the horrible writing. What can I say? It's the best I can do.

I quickly fold the paper and turn to greet the doctors. There's a whole group of them today. They're laughing as they bunch through the door. The minute they see me they stop and look serious. I guess it's an inside joke. No doubt I wouldn't understand.

They step aside to let Dr. Granger speak to me first. Not that any of them ever says anything. They just glare and try to look interested.

Since when did the vocational counselor join the tour? He looks a little out of place with his golf shirt and cords compared to the others in their white smocks. The pharmacist holds her Bible in crossed arms in front of her chest and whispers quietly out the side of her mouth to the resident doctor. The director of nursing stands importantly with the two doctors, and the head nurse smiles apologetically at me. She's the only one who tries to make me feel comfortable.

"Well, Miss Parker, how are you today?" Dr. Granger says as he chairs the floor.

"Fine, thank you," I say, feeling small and uncomfortable.

"How's the bladder coming along?"

I've said all I'm allowed. The director of nursing jumps in after looking at her chart.

"There doesn't seem to be any change, doctor. Her expressions are still only one hundred cc's and she has a high residual."

"How many times is she incontinent during the day?"

I feel myself sinking into my chair. The vocational counselor looks out the window.

"On an average, only twice."

"Hmmm," he says and writes something in his notes. "What's this I see about a request to see a gynecologist? Are you having problems?"

I push my chair back. They're standing too close.

"I..."

The head nurse tries to save me.

"I have made an appointment with Dr. Young. He is coming to see Sally on Friday afternoon. She is interested in knowing the possibilities of ever having a family. Dr. Young is going to give her an examination and discuss the matter with her."

"I see." The doctor turns to me. "I would think you would have enough on your mind. You know you are going to be quite busy looking after yourself. A family would be very difficult. I hope you're not thinking about this in the near future."

"No," I stutter, wishing they would fade into the walls. "I'm only interested."

"Fine. Well, then, I think it's a good idea."

He leaves and the group follows him out the door. I don't know whether the pain in my stomach is from hunger or humiliation.

20

ERICSON LOOKS TIRED. He has dark circles under his eyes, and even though the weather has been good all summer, his skin is pale. I realize that I know very little about this man, that we always talk about me.

"Are you feeling all right?" I ask.

"I'm fine," he answers. He notices my interest and continues, "My wife has been away for the summer and I've been looking after our two children. They have been running me a little ragged." He smiles. "It shows?"

"You don't look terrible, only a bit tired. You look hot. You should really have a window." I chuckle to myself, thinking of all the times I've wished there was a window in this room.

"That would be nice. Tell me, how did it go with Dr. Young?"

I immediately look away.

"Fine." I know that if I can talk to anybody about this it will be Ericson. After all, he was the one who suggested the visit in the first place.

I don't know how to start.

"He was a nice man."

Ericson pushes delicately.

"Did he tell you what you wanted to know?"

I want to tell him so I catch my breath.

"Yes. He said there shouldn't be any problems if I want to have a baby. He gave me an examination and said everything looked normal." My words tumble over one another, but I'm glad I've begun. It's getting easier to talk. "He said that they would keep a close watch over me and that there was no reason to worry any more than one would with a normal pregnancy. Of course, there is a possibility that the delivery would be a cesarean section, but that that was nothing to worry about."

Ericson looks pleased, even though a frown wrinkles his wide forehead.

"You don't sound totally convinced."

I don't want to tell Ericson what I think. Yes, I'm convinced. But somehow I don't feel as happy as I thought I would. It makes me feel whole, or partially whole. But now that I know it's possible, the whole idea scares me.

How can I be thinking about having a baby when I don't even have anyone who loves me?

I feel as though I've been racing down a dark tunnel. When I reach the end I come into the light, only to be enclosed again in blackness.

"It doesn't sound as if they know very much about it," I say slowly. "You know, I used to think doctors knew everything, but I'm beginning to find out that isn't so."

"No one knows everything, least of all doctors. There is too much to know. At least it sounds positive."

"Yes, and I really don't have to worry about it for a while, do I?"

Ericson shakes his head. He doesn't look so tired when his eyes shine.

"No, you don't."

"You know, Brian likes kids. He'd like to have lots of them, as many as he could afford."

Ericson wants to know more about Brian. He knows I'm touchy, but he manages to say the right thing to get me talking. So I tell him about that weekend, how Mother didn't want us to go, and how I told her I was going anyway. I tell him about the skiing, about the lodge, about how close I felt to Brian, and finally, about the accident.

My words hurt as my throat closes up on me. I force them out. I want to finish, to tell it all. Tightness stings my eyes and stretches across my forehead like a rubber band. I know the story so well that the painful words come hard and fast.

"You see, it's all my fault. I have to accept the blame."

I hang my head and clench my teeth. I'm aware of Ericson leaning forward over his desk, trying to get as close to me as possible. His words are tender.

"No one blames you, Sally."

"I do. Look what I've done to myself." I can't hold

back any longer, and large drops roll freely down my face. "Why did I do it?" My body heaves.

"Sally, sometimes things happen without reason. No one is to blame, they just happen."

"But look what I've done to my family," I sob. "I've hurt everyone who loves me."

"Sally, your accident has hurt you very deeply. Of course those who love you are going to hurt with you."

"And Brian. He tried so hard to help me, to love me and be with me, but I turned him away. I didn't want to hurt him and I've only hurt him more. I didn't want him to waste his life."

Ericson sits back. I can see him relax.

"I think you should let Brian decide about his own life. What about your life? Don't you think it's time you started saving your own life?"

I wipe at my face with the back of my hand. I don't even care that I've cried in front of Ericson.

"You know, I've tried to push Brian out of my thoughts, but he's always there. It's been like trying to block the sunshine, shut out music. I thought I was doing okay with Jake. He was special and I really did care for him. We needed each other. But I knew it would never be the same, that I would never totally understand him. In the end all I did was compare him to Brian."

I feel as though I've opened all the doors on a spring day, and thoughts of Brian are rushing in like a fresh breeze. He is in the air and as I breathe in I feel light and tingly.

"Oh, I've missed him so much. I wish I could see him."

"Why can't you?"

"I sent him away. He told me he wouldn't come back until I stopped feeling sorry for myself, until I called him."

Ericson sits quietly, letting me hear my own words.

"But I do feel sorry for myself. I'll always feel sorry and wish this never happened."

"Sally, there is a difference between feeling sad about something that has happened in your life and using that sadness to thrash out at those around you."

* * *

Back in my room I wait at the window, watching for Michael. One day he saw me and waved. Ever since then he always looks and we wave. It's become a ritual.

I realize I don't feel resentful of the staff going home, leaving us behind. After all, isn't it enough that they've chosen a career to help us? If I ever get out of this mess I think I'll become a therapist.

I laugh out loud. I mean, look at my fantastic background!

Suddenly I notice a white envelope tucked under the corner of my radio.

A letter! I grab at it and quickly flip it over. In the corner the return address is New Zealand. I push at it and then with both hands I raise it to my mouth. I tear at the envelope with my teeth and spit the little pieces of paper out. Biting at the corner, I manage to pull the letter out.

It's a card, and on the cover is a picture of a plump nurse all dressed in white. Inside, the writing is neat and round.

September 28, 1973

Dear Sally,

I was so delighted to receive your letter. Of course I don't mind hearing from you, silly. Don't ever think that again.

I have been thinking about you so much and wondering how you are. Your letter was so long and newsy and your writing isn't bad at all. It certainly has improved from the days at City.

I had to laugh at your description of doctors' rounds — how true. I read it to Bob and he promises to try and be better. If so he'll win first prize.

We absolutely love living here in New Zealand. No, it is not as beautiful as all the pictures. It is twice as beautiful and the weather is glorious. I don't have much of a tan though because it is so nice every day, sun tanning is not a big item. (I'm glad to hear that you have had a hot summer and that you have managed to get into the sunshine. I remember how brown you were the day we met. No wonder your love life seems so active. Jake? Michael?)

You ask about Bob. Oh, Sally, I am just bursting to tell you. He is truly wonderful and I realize what a sap I've been. He is very thoughtful and a dream to live with. Can you imagine, he is neat and loves doing the dishes. He is working very hard at the hospital putting in many long hours. At first I was quite lonely and missed the hospital dreadfully (and the wonderful patients like you). However, now I value my free time and have been able to do some studying. I have become very interested in midwifery (which reminds me of something else I want to talk to you about) and have been doing a lot of reading on it.

Anyway, back to Bob. Hold on to your chair—we are getting married! I've known all along that he was the only man I could ever love but I was afraid to commit myself for a lifetime. The whole idea was so frightening to me. And, Sally, I have you to thank. You were the one who made me realize that we can't shut out the ones we love. I am so happy I am delirious. We are going to come home to be married next summer. It will be a small wedding with family and a few close friends.

I have something very special to ask you. Would you like to be my maid of honor? You would make Bob and me very happy if you say yes. His younger brother, Harry, is to be the best man. Please think about it and let me know as soon as you can.

Now, I have a few things to ask you. I wish so much that I could be with you and talk with you. Why haven't you seen Brian? Remember, you sent him away. Do me one favor. Ask yourself a question. Do you still love him? If your answer is yes, phone him. Don't make the same mistake I almost did.

The second thing is, Hooray! How wonderful to know that you can still have a child. I've talked to a few of Bob's *friends and they too think there is little reason why you couldn't. I've decided to look into it a little further. I will send you the results of my findings.*

Sal, I must dash. Bob comes home for supper but only has an hour so everything must be ready. Keep up the good work in physio and write me as soon as you get the chance.

I miss you.

Love,
Rosey

I realize I'm crying, and I wipe at my tears with my sleeve. Quickly I turn back to find the words, *I have something very special to ask you. Would you like to be my maid of honor?*

I can't believe it. I read it over and over. Does she really want me to be in her wedding? I cry harder than I have in a long time. I am actually bawling.

All at once I see Michael waving below. I raise my arm and wave. I'm still crying, but I am so happy. The tears running down my cheeks and into my mouth are sweet and warm.

The next day I feel great as I wheel through the waiting room, barely aware of the carpet, and into the physio room. In a matter of minutes I transfer myself onto the mats and sit with my hands stretched behind me holding myself up. I watch Michael fondly as he walks toward me. I love the way he looks, so strong and yet huggable. We grin at one another.

"Hi, Sally. You look awfully happy today. Or," he glances down at himself, "is it something I'm wearing?"

I laugh, "No, dummy. I just feel good."

"Great. Then we'll get lots of work out of you today." Michael kneels on the mats beside me and begins the routine exercises.

"Guess what," I say. "Do you remember my friend Rosey? The one I told you about who was a nurse at City."

"Yes. She went to New Zealand?"

"She's getting married and she asked me to be her maid of honor." I am disappointed by Michael's lack of response. "I can't believe she actually wants me."

"Okay, now, push with your shoulder across your chest. Don't let me stop you. Good." There is a silence except for his commands. "I don't see what's so strange about that."

I push hard. "You wouldn't." I think about the reception, the dresses, and what about the pictures?

"Are you ready to roll today? Get up a good swing and don't forget to use your head."

My shoulder lifts off — then I fall back on the mat.

"Michael," I continue, "it's just that I find it hard to believe someone could like me enough, knowing what I am. I mean, I feel like a child, or as if I'm in a different class or something."

"You shouldn't feel that way." Michael sits cross-legged beside me. "Now, I'm not going to help you. Roll," he commands in a friendly manner.

On the third try I fling my arms with all my might, throw my head as hard as I can, and over I go.

I can't believe it. After all this time I have actually rolled.

"That's my girl," Michael slaps me on the back. "Fantastic. I knew you could do it."

"Let me do it again." I let myself flop onto my back, fling my arms and over I go. I do it again and again until I'm dizzy with joy.

"Now that you've got yourself on your side, see if you can pull yourself up into a sitting position."

By reaching down and hooking my wrist under my thigh, I pull my body down toward my legs and manage to pull myself up.

"It's easy," I sing out. "You told me I could do it, but I never believed you. I think now that I can do anything as long as I keep trying."

I feel light and marvelous, and I want to jump up and down and tell everybody I can roll. But most of all I want to give Michael a great big kiss. He is as happy as I am, and we smile at each other. I know he wants to hug me, too.

My heart is pounding as I cling to the awkward moment, not knowing what to do or say but not wanting it to end.

"Sally, I love you for trying so hard, and for winning. I'm glad I know you."

There are elves dancing in the pit of my stomach. I hold his words, treasure them like something precious. I know now that this is the beginning of everything.

"Okay, smarty." His eyes are flashing. "Get yourself up. From now on you're doing all the work."

As I wheel through the department I can't stop smiling. I notice that everyone else is smiling back at me. I see people as I have never seen them before. Have they always been there?

21

I SIT IN FRONT of the mirror looking long and hard at myself.

I know I'm not the same person I was. I look different. I examine my features one by one: my eyes, my nose, my mouth. They are all the same. My hair is different. Is that what makes me look changed, or is it the fact that I'm sitting down?

No, it's something else. I lean forward, trying to get closer to the glass, but the sink juts into my stomach and stops me. I look down at the sink and then back to my eyes.

I have it. All I can see is my front. I never see all of me.

Is it because I've stopped feeling that I've stopped looking?

But I haven't stopped feeling, I tell myself sharply. I can still feel inside my toes, my legs, inside my gut. Maybe I feel too much.

I think about Michael. I remember the look in his eyes when I sat up, how happy he was for me – how happy I was for myself.

That's it. It's joy that's been missing. I have been alive but I felt no joy.

I laugh out loud at my silly grin. I feel as if I've been on a rollercoaster ride. The first hill is always the worst, the hills get steeper and the car goes faster, but the ride is easier closer to the end. You just learn to hold on.

Thank you, Michael, I whisper. Thank you for making me whole. I wish I could spend the rest of my life with you, but that would be too easy.

Ericson is right. I have been thrashing out my hate and anger to hurt those around me. I guess I wanted everyone to suffer with me — the doctors, nurses, therapists, and the people I'm supposed to love.

There's nothing wrong with this place. It's hard to remember that when you have to be here.

I hope they understand. I want them to realize that I haven't meant it, that I am thankful.

There's got to be something out in the world for me after all. I still want to love and be loved. I can. I know it. I know I can't be pampered for the rest of my life. I've got to get on with it myself.

I'm glad they let me be angry, that they left me alone to fight with myself. It must have been so hard for my mother to let me fight her. To put up with my refusal to go home, to let her help me or even to see me.

I may have lost Brian. I don't see how he can understand all this. I want to be good and fun to be with. I don't want to feel sorry for myself anymore.

I know now what I have to do.

"You'll make out better if you do something with that face," I say to my reflection in the mirror.

I reach for my small bag of makeup. I know he won't be able to see me — it will be my voice that counts — but I want to look my best.

I have to wait for the phone. It's being used. I don't dare move or think. I don't want to change my mind so I sit and stare. I don't even practice what I'm going to say. It doesn't really matter.

Finally, I ask the nurse to dial for me.

Give it to me. Don't wait to hear it ring, I think impatiently with a lump beating hard in my chest. I want to hear him say hello.

"Brian?"

"Speaking."

God, he doesn't know me.

I say meekly, "It's Sally."

"Sally!" There is silence. My heart stops. I can't speak. His words come slowly. "Sally, how are you?"

"Fine," I choke out. Again there is silence. "Brian?"

"What is it, Sally? Are you all right?"

"Will..." I swallow, "will you come and see me?"

"Are you sure you want me to?"

"Yes. Please, Brian."

"When?"

"Tomorrow?"

"I can't come tomorrow, but maybe on Thursday. Around seven?"

"That will be fine."

He's so far away. I want to pull him through the phone. To touch him, hold him, to feel his arms around me. I want to cry into his shoulder, to tell him I've missed him. I want to tell him Jake is gone, that I can roll, and have babies.

But I only say, "I'll see you then. Goodbye."

The second call is easier.

"Mom?"

"Hi, darling. I thought you were going to the show?"

"I decided not to."

"Are you all right?" Her voice is suddenly anxious.

I laugh. "Yes, Mom, I'm fine. Mom? Do you think I could come home for Thanksgiving?"

"Of course, honey, we were expecting you."

"No, I mean for the whole weekend." There is silence on the other end of the phone. I know she is crying, too. "Could you ask Dad to pick me up?"

"Yes, oh, yes."

"Guess what. Brian's coming to see me Thursday."

"Did he phone you?" Her words are still shaky.

"No, I phoned him."

"Sally, I'm glad."

"Yes," I sigh softly, "so am I."

Acknowledgments

Thank you to Peggy Kent for her guidance in writing this novel.

Thank you to GF Strong Rehabilitation Centre and all those who helped me through my own rehabilitation.

Thank you to my husband, family and friends for their constant love and encouragement.

Afterword

Our mum, Sandi Richmond (Sally), was an amazing woman. People always ask what it was like to grow up with a quadriplegic mother. "Pretty normal," we always say. She swam, sailed, raised two boy terrors and came to every school and sporting event.

She also had an incredible talent for bringing people together, like at the annual Sandi Richmond Christmas party. After losing her eleven years ago to a five-year battle with breast cancer, we have continued this tradition. Every year a speech is delivered in her honor: "The reason we are all here tonight is because Sandi has touched our lives in some way..." The eighty guests celebrate as if she were right alongside us, with jokes, games, cocktails, stories — and the always popular tacky Christmas sweaters. For many it is the only time they see each other all year, and yet they would not miss it. This is not just a party. It represents the true essence of what Sandi lived and fought so hard for: family, friends, food, wine, sharing, good times, and to really be thankful for all that we have.

As Sandi's children, we are now raising awareness and money to support breast cancer research for the BC Cancer Society through the Weekend to End Breast Cancer. We do this sixty-kilometer walk with the spirit, costumes and laughs that would make our mum proud. Royalties from this new edition of *Wheels for Walking* will be donated to the BC Cancer Society and GF Strong Rehabilitation Centre's spinal research program, in recognition of all their support and dedication to Sandi and so many other people with cancer or spinal injuries.

We hope our mum's story will continue to be a source of inspiration for others.

Jim and Mike Richmond